Dead Man Blues

DEAD MAN BLUES

A NOVEL

S. D. House

NEW YORK

Books should be disposed of and recycled according to local requirements. All paper materials used are FSC compliant.

This is a work of fiction. All of the names, characters, organizations, places, and events portrayed in this novel are either products of the author's imagination or are used fictitiously. Any resemblance to real or actual events, locales, or persons, living or dead, is entirely coincidental.

Copyright © 2025 by S. D. House

All rights reserved.

Published in the United States by Crooked Lane Books, an imprint of The Quick Brown Fox & Company LLC.

Crooked Lane Books and its logo are trademarks of The Quick Brown Fox & Company LLC.

Library of Congress Catalog-in-Publication data available upon request.

ISBN (hardcover): 979-8-89242-348-9
ISBN (paperback): 979-8-89242-349-6
ISBN (ebook): 979-8-89242-350-2

Cover design by Ashton Smith

Printed in the United States.

www.crookedlanebooks.com

Crooked Lane Books
34 West 27th St., 10th Floor
New York, NY 10001

First Edition: October 2025

The authorized representative in the EU for product safety and compliance is eucomply OÜPärnu mnt 139b-14, 11317 Tallinn, Estonia, hello@eucompliancepartner.com, +33757690241

10 9 8 7 6 5 4 3 2 1

*For my cousins,
who love the lake as much as I do:
Dena, Eleshia, Gina, Lisa,
Melanie, and Nancy*

Prologue

Esau Campbell, after several years of wandering and messing up, felt like a lost puzzle piece that's finally been rescued from underneath the couch and nudged into its proper place. His success at running this fishing camp had been helped along no small amount when the world- record largemouth bass had been caught here four years ago.

These two things—Esau's success and the world record—went hand in hand because, unbeknownst to anyone, Esau had slid two dozen metal sinkers down the gullet of the big ole bass when the fisherman brought it in to be weighed. Esau knew that fish was big enough to maybe be on the list, which would bring in a whole lot more business and secure his job, which he needed badly. But Esau wanted to guarantee it, so he dropped in the sinkers, then called in a notary to witness him weighing the bass. The affidavit was signed and made official at a staggering twenty-two pounds and two ounces.

A world record.

And that had sealed the deal not only for the Capability Fishing Camp but also for Cedar Lake itself. Business had been booming ever since despite the whispers of some fishermen who suspected Esau of subterfuge.

Esau always liked to use the shower house late at night, when all the guests had already turned in, and this night he had played a lengthy poker game with some of the boys staying at the camp and had gotten a little too drunk, so he needed a cold shower to sober him up and wash off some of the day's stink.

The day had been a long one for him. He had mucked out all the nightcrawler basins at the bait shop, then filled them with new dirt. He'd drained, scrubbed, and refilled the minnow tanks. Like always he had tended to the camp guests all day long, and last he had climbed up onto his cottage roof to add a couple of shingles after finding a small leak a couple days before. Once up there, he stumbled, and when he went to correct himself, he pulled a muscle that had become more inflamed as the night dragged on. Sitting hunched at the game of cards certainly hadn't helped, but he had been winning, so he wasn't about to quit. By the time the men all left at two-thirty that morning, the small of his back ached as if a hot brick was sitting at the base of his spine.

So Esau whistled softly as he padded down the flagstone path to the shower house. He looked out onto the still lake, its calm waters lit by more stars than he'd ever seen before, brighter in the moonless sky. This was the prettiest, most peaceful place in the world, he thought, and he wanted to stay here the rest of his life. He heard a whippoorwill call and stopped for a moment to hear it repeat its lonesome cry. He had always identified with that pining sound.

Once inside he took off his clothes, hung them on the small silver hook on the wall, and turned the water up to as hot as it would go. Immediately steam pumped out along with the stinging stream. Already the heat pounding into the small of his back was working its magic. He leaned one hand against the wall and let the needles of water pound against his muscles, becoming so relaxed that he closed his eyes and leaned his forehead against the cool concrete blocks.

Something made him open his eyes. He didn't know what. Not a movement or a sound really, but a change in the way the air felt.

Then he saw: the electricity had gone out. The lights in here had been dim to start with, but now there was thick darkness. All he could make out around him was the steam slithering through the shower house. Probably one of the boys messing with him.

"Hey, you sons of bitches," he hollered. "Cut it out now."

Esau put his hands out in front of him, not exactly sure if he was feeling for someone nearby or if he was simply trying to find the wall to guide him over to the light switch.

And then, he realized someone was within inches of him, their shape sudden and looming. Before he could even speak, the first slash of the knife swiped through his right side and he felt blood—slicker and thicker than the water—stream down his leg.

His hand found purchase on the shoulder of this intruder, but he didn't even have time to sink his fingers into the meat there before the knife pierced his heart. Esau gasped, then sank to his knees, both hands around the knife now, trying to pull it out. If he could get it out, he'd be okay, he thought.

But Esau fell face-first onto the concrete floor, plunging the knife an inch deeper and ending his troubled life that had only recently found its footing. The force threw him to his side and he collapsed that way. Just before death completely took over, he could feel the water from the showerhead pecking at his eyeballs and he wanted to call out for his mother and Celeste, but just as he put his lips together to form the first sound, he was gone.

Chapter 1

Just about all Dave had left after the divorce were his books; his wiener dog, Shorty; a whole crate of record albums; and his houseboat, which he called *The Sherlock*. Once he'd had the biggest house on Main Street, the most important job in town (mayor), the prettiest and unhappiest wife, two cars, and the only privately owned television set in the entire town of Shady Grove. Even his job had been taken from him. Not that he had wanted to keep it anyway. But *still*.

He'd had it all and now he only had what he really needed, but best of all was having a quiet place to live, right here on Cedar Lake.

As he sat on the porch of *The Sherlock*, looking out at the black water and the starry night sky, with Shorty in his lap, a glass of Jameson Irish whiskey in his hand, and Bessie Smith playing on the record player behind him, he knew he didn't need a thing more.

"Nobody knows you when you're down and out," Bessie sang, and that's exactly why he loved her: she always told the pure-D straight truth, no holds barred. The thing was that he didn't even mind that nobody from his old life came around anymore. He had a few new friends here at the marina after only six months of living on *The Sherlock*. They were the misfits, the outcasts, the ones who didn't fit in back in town, but Dave reckoned that's who he had always been, too. He'd been fooling himself and everybody else when he'd been the most popular citizen of Shady Grove. The truth was this: Dave didn't like many people. When he did like someone, he really liked them, but he had decided long ago that for the most part, the world was full of assholes.

"A toast," Dave said, holding up his second glass of whiskey toward the night sky, "to this night. To the fourteenth night of June 1955, a night that I have to put up with no assholes. Here's mud in your eye, June fourteenth!" He tipped back his head and the whiskey slid down, warm and oaky and honeyed.

Dave wasn't normally a drinker. He certainly wasn't an alcoholic. But some nights he couldn't stop thinking about Germany. He couldn't stop thinking about all those bodies, all those skeletons walking toward him with their arms stretched out, asking for help. He couldn't stop thinking about his buddies who had died beside him while he, miraculously, had lived. Other nights he couldn't stop thinking about the way his best friend and his wife had betrayed him. He knew that in some strange way he was just as haunted by that as he was by the atrocities he had witnessed in Europe. Both sets of events were about the cruelty people can do to each other: one was on an epic scale and the other intimate. So, some nights he sat on the porch and watched the night sky and had a few glasses of Jameson, petting Shorty and listening to music until he could go to sleep.

He'd had both things on his mind all day because he had been alone since early morning. He had borrowed Rex's runabout and gone out on the lake, just driving around, stopping for an occasional swim in the clean, deep water. He had laid in the boat, reading the latest Erle Stanley Gardner, and then for at least an hour he had dozed, awaking to find himself a bit sunburned before heading back into the marina.

Suddenly Shorty's hackles went up and a low cough caught in the back of her throat. Shorty was very small, but she didn't realize this, so she was always ready to go on the defense for Dave, who hadn't heard a thing. Shorty sprang up on her short legs and stood in hunting pose—front right paw held up—and let out a riot of barking. She was so agitated that a rumbling growl spread through her chest when Dave went to calm her.

A light went on in the houseboat next door, which was especially strange since nobody lived on it. Rex Hardy, who owned the marina and half the boats moored here, had been trying to sell it for the last year.

Shorty really went crazy then, struggling to jump down so she could rip out the ankle meat of the intruder next door.

"Shorty, Shorty, calm down, baby!" Dave cooed. "It's okay! It's all right." He wasn't sure if it was all right or not, actually. Perhaps someone was prowling about on the little houseboat next door.

But then the door opened on the boat porch next to him and the silhouette of a woman stepped out. "It's okay, sweetie," she said, and Shorty instantly switched gears and wagged her tail as if this new woman might be the bearer of very good treats. Shorty stood on her hind legs, leaning against the railing so she could see over to the other porch. She even gave a small pitiful whine, the way she did when she wanted to be picked up. The woman was lost to the shadows as she stepped closer to the railings separating their porches. She leaned over to pat Shorty's head and Dave could see the soft curve of her face, the bright silky auburn of her hair. There was something very familiar about her.

"You've got a good little watch doggie there," she said, then brought her eyes up to latch on his. The woman kept her right hand busy with rubbing at Shorty's chest while the dog reared back with her eyes half closed in ecstasy, and extended her other one for a handshake. Then he could see her face: Nina Owens. A face he hadn't seen in twenty-five years. But he had thought of her on occasion and always missed her.

"I'm your new neighbor, I guess," she said. She didn't seem to recognize him in the darkness. "I rented this old beauty yesterday."

"Nina," Dave said, his voice full of disbelief, remembering all their time playing together as kids. Running through the woods. Building a dam in the creek. That innocent kiss, a peck on the lips that had been the first for both of them. Watching as her parents' truck drove away, taking Nina away from him. "It's me. It's Dave."

"Dave? Wh—Dave Hendricks?" she said, her smile overtaking her face. "I can't believe it!" She broke into a full, contagious laugh, and he joined in. "I knew I'd run into you eventually, but I didn't figure I'd land right beside you."

They had been best friends until they were ten years old, when her parents had been forced off their land for the flooding of the lake. A deep woods had separated Dave's family land from Nina's, and that grove of trees—along with the ridge they stood on—had kept Dave's family's property safe from the taking. But Nina's family had to move off the land their people had lived on since the early 1800s. Her father had been so angry about it that he left the state altogether. Nina had promised to write from their new home in Alabama, but she had only sent a couple letters and had never answered the last one he wrote to her. Dave wasn't about to admit to her now how that had hurt him, how he had pined for her a couple of years, how he had always wondered where she was.

Dave watched her there in the shadows, laughing, and thought he was going to like having her as a neighbor just fine. Shorty seemed to agree.

"What are you doing back?" he asked, trying to mask the amazement in his voice.

She leaned against the metal railings between them. Shorty stood on her hind legs, licking at Nina's hands. She didn't seem to mind. In fact, she didn't even seem to notice.

"Well, I've worked in newspapers all over the South but never have been satisfied anywhere. So when I saw an opening here, I just thought what the hell, I'll go back to Shawnee County. My family never did get over this place."

Dave had been small when the community conversations had started about the lake taking over the valley, but he remembered how heated the community meetings had become. No one had been more upset than Nina's father. Legend had it he had once pulled a gun on the Corps of Engineers men who came to give him final notice that his family had to leave, an order of eminent domain in hand. The Corps had paid top dollar for the property but still, most people didn't want to leave land that had been in their families for generations.

"Well, I never did get over y'all leaving," Dave said, and let out a little laugh because he hadn't meant to say it out loud.

"What a coincidence!" Nina said quickly, as if embarrassed by what he had said. "To be your neighbor again."

"So you're working for *The Shady Grove Sentinel*?"

"Yep. Lead reporter of the smallest paper in the state. I'm in the big time now, huh?"

"At least you're employed."

"You're not? I thought you were the mayor."

Dave wondered how she knew that. Maybe she had missed him, too. The album had reached its end and there was nothing but the comforting sound of the lapping water between them.

"Well, I was. For seven years. And sheriff for two years before that."

"What happened?" Nina sat on one of the rickety metal folding chairs that had stood on the empty porch of the houseboat for the last year, waiting for someone to unfold it.

"The short version is that I was happy as a person could be, I thought. Loved my little town. Loved serving its people. Loved my wife. I thought we had it made. But then I found out she was sleeping with the town sheriff, who happened to be my own best friend."

"Oh God. I'm sorry, Dave."

"Yep." Dave felt around on the floor beside his chair. "This calls for a drink." He held up the green bottle of Jameson. "Join me?"

"You go ahead," she said. "I drank too much at supper and had to get sobered up from that, so I don't want to drink again."

"Sure?"

"I'm more of a gin girl, anyway."

"I'm sorry, I don't have any of that in stock," he said, "but your new landlord, Rex, specializes in it."

"Oh, please, drink up," she said, throwing a dismissive hand toward him. "Don't worry about me."

"All right, I will," Dave said, and tipped back his glass. The whiskey soaked into his tongue. "I'll drink for both of us. It's not often I drink, but I don't have anywhere to go tonight."

"Forgive me if this is too personal, but I am a reporter, so—"

"Ask me anything," Dave said.

"How does your wife having an affair lead to you not having a job?"

"Because the night I found out I had too much of this," Dave said, and held up the glass of whiskey. "And then

I stupidly got into my car. And stupidly drove it into the county courthouse."

"Ah, I see," Nina said, nodding. "You never did do anything halfway, even as a little boy."

"And your newspaper had a field day with that, then the other papers got on board and well, I finally resigned. So I went from being the town mayor to being the town screw-up."

"I've always preferred the screw-ups, myself," Nina said.

"You're kind to say so," Dave said. "But to tell you the truth, I'm happier now than I've ever been. I didn't even realize how miserable I was. I was just floating through life, making money and buying Janet whatever she wanted and not even noticing that she didn't care anything about me."

"Janet was your wife?"

Dave nodded.

"Not Janet Dawson?"

"The one and only."

"We hated her in elementary school. She was a snob even when she was ten years old!"

"Well, I thought she had changed. But she hadn't. I don't know what I was thinking. I was really good at basketball in high school and that caused her to bat her big blue eyes at me one day. One thing led to another and—"

"And the next thing you know," Nina offered, "you're married to the cheerleading captain, you're mayor of the town, and don't really have control of your own life."

"Exactly," Dave replied. But how did she know Janet had been the cheerleading captain in high school? Something told him Nina had been keeping up with things since she had been gone. Maybe she had already known he had been married to Janet and was just playing along like she didn't. Or maybe it was a lucky guess. Even in elementary school it had been apparent that Janet would grow up to be the most popular girl in school.

"My life hasn't exactly gone the way I planned either, Dave," Nina said, but she didn't offer any more information. "I reckon it's that way for most folks."

"Well, if life wasn't full of surprises, it'd be awful dull." Dave looked out at the calm lake.

"I always wondered about you, during the war," Nina said. "I have to admit that when the war was over, I snooped around some. Easy to do when you're with the newspaper. I did some investigating to make sure you came back."

Dave took the last drink of whiskey from his glass. *No more of that*, he thought, because he was definitely starting to buzz.

"I did come back," he said. "Got hailed as a war hero by Shady Grove, although I hadn't done anything particularly heroic. Came home and ran for sheriff even though I didn't have a lick of experience, and I won. I was more surprised than anybody."

"I can't imagine how bad the war was," Nina said.

"No, you can't," Dave said, a little sharper than he intended. There was a flash in his mind of the bodies, stacked like firewood, the people emerging from the smoke and ash, the eerie silence of the day they liberated the camp.

"My dad was in the Great War, remember? He never did get over it."

He did remember. Her father hadn't dealt well with the shell shock. Growing up, Dave had often heard people say how Old Man Owens never was right after coming back from France. And once his land was taken by the government, that anger seemed to be on the surface all the time instead of simply being a boil that rose up occasionally. Sometimes Dave and Nina had played out in those woods together because both of them were trying to get away from their fathers: hers raging from the war he couldn't shed and his full of the anger that whiskey stoked in him. They had understood this about each other as children without having to articulate it much at all. That's one reason he had missed her so badly when she left; nobody else got it the way she did. There was something about living in an angry house that bound people.

He found himself laughing in a way he hadn't in a long time. Still, there was something a little off, something he couldn't quite put his finger on, but it mostly felt like distrust. There was something this woman was hiding. Dave reckoned he was probably being arrogant in wondering if she was talking nonstop because she was nervous about seeing him again. She said she'd moved back to Shady Grove four days ago to take a job for the local newspaper, had been staying at the Town Square Hotel. She didn't like any of the rental properties in town, and had heard about the houseboat for rent down at the marina.

"I took a look at it yesterday and I never considered living on a houseboat before in my life, but I kind of fell in love with the idea of being on the water," she said.

She had been married right out of college, she told him, but it only lasted a couple years and hadn't produced any children. "I don't have any intention of ever doing *that* again," she said, but didn't expand on why it had been such a bad experience.

Dave felt that familiar grief wash through his stomach when he thought about both of them being childless. He had always wanted a baby so badly. The whole time he had been in Europe, he had consoled himself by thinking that he would survive the war, go back home and marry Janet, and they'd have two kids, the American dream. That's what had kept him going. And now he not only didn't have any kids, he didn't have any of it at all.

As Nina went on, he found out they had even more in common: they both loved Sherlock Holmes, Ella Fitzgerald, and Yorkshire tea. Dave had picked up the habit of afternoon tea during his time stationed in England and did it even more religiously now that he lived so close to Rex, who was from England. Nina's only explanation was that she needed it to calm down after work.

"Five years ago, I had an aneurysm and almost died," she said.

"So young?"

"They can happen anytime," she said. "I'm telling you, Dave, I really did die for a few minutes. I saw a big bright light, saw my mother waiting at the end of a tunnel, the whole shebang. I thought I had left this earth forever. That'll change you."

Before he could respond, Nina yawned and glanced at her watch. "Oh my lord, it's five in the morning!" Nina laughed. "I guess we really did some catching up."

Dave never had a chance to reply. From across the widest part of Cedar Lake, there came anguished screams, curling through the warm night air over the still water. Dave figured the sound was coming from the direction of the fish camp, and he was surprised by the clarity of the screams. Open water was an amazing carrier of sound, and the yelling was so piercing that both he and Nina were startled and they both turned to look that way.

"We need to go over there," Dave said.

"What's over there?"

"Capability Fishing Camp," he said.

"Is there a little boat we can take?" Nina asked. "I don't imagine these houseboats have much horsepower."

"Rex won't mind if we take his," Dave said, already on his feet.

Chapter 2

The screaming was coming from Ronald Rose, who was visiting from the North with his wife, Denise. They had planned on getting on the road to Alabama early this morning, and so he had arisen groggy and foul-tempered, grabbed a towel and some toiletries, and had stumbled out to the shower house, where he found the body of Esau Campbell.

He had been surprised to find that the lights didn't respond when he turned them on at the switch by the door. He could hear a shower running and thought that someone must have left it on just for meanness. He clicked the light switch a couple more times, stupidly thinking that might fix the problem, but of course it didn't. He had brought his flashlight to make his way down the path from their cottage up on the hillside, but he knew he couldn't shower and hold it in this darkness. Still, something felt off. He clicked on the flashlight and scanned the room with its beam.

By the time his light had swept past the first corner, the brightness fell on the stream of steaming water and the person lying on the floor beneath it. Maybe they had slipped and fallen onto the concrete. Or maybe a heart attack. Whatever the case, something was wrong.

This was no slip, no heart attack.

There was a wide gash in the man's side, where a peaceful stream of blood was making its ways toward the floor drain.

There was a knife in his heart.

Strangely enough, Ron wasn't so much horrified by what he saw as he was by the memories that all came back to him. What he had seen as a little boy. *The blood. The knife.* He felt as if he was swimming back from the bottom of very black water, as if he might have been sleepwalking until this moment.

There was a moment when he didn't even think about the murderer maybe still being in the shower house. He could hear the pummeling water, could see the rolling steam. He could even smell the metallic tang of blood in the air, the moldy scent of a damp place. But in his mind he was back there, thirty years ago, his mother's bloody body lying in front of him. That's why he screamed.

Then a jagged bolt of fright ran up his back and he drew the beam of light in a circle around him, checking all corners for whomever had done this. *Empty. Empty. Empty.* He couldn't run. But he moved out of there fast, his screams morphing into a cry for help until he saw the others running toward him.

Chapter 3

Dave and Nina made it across the misty lake in only ten minutes, pushing the little johnboat as hard as it would go. The warm wind of the summer night felt so good washing over them that Dave closed his eyes in satisfaction.

"I don't know what we think we'll do when we get there," Nina said as they neared the fish camp. The dock lights melted across the water in jagged yellow lines.

"Well, we couldn't sit there and do nothing while someone screamed bloody murder," Dave replied.

By the time they reached the small dock at the fish camp, all was silent. As Dave tied up the boat, he could see that two men stood near the cinderblock shower house, looking down at a woman sitting on the ground next to a man who sat on his haunches, his face in his hands. All of them were shrouded in the mist steaming down out of the hunchbacked mountain and made into silhouettes by a single tall streetlamp that stood in the middle of the camp.

Behind them the mountain was solid black, but the sky was lightening from the deep blue of full night into a rose-tinted gray that announced morning would be there within the hour.

Dave was surprised to see a woman here as this fish camp was used by men focused on catching as many fish as possible. They came in the hopes of snagging one to rival the world record and to escape their wives and lives back home. Right now the two men were mumbling to each other as they leaned over a body sprawled on the concrete near the entrance. All Dave could see at first were a pair of bare feet sticking out from between the men's legs, but when he approached, they stepped back to allow him in so he saw everything. Perhaps they thought he was an official in some capacity. The body language of the sheriff he had once been was hard to lose, Dave reckoned.

There lay a dead man, naked except for a bath towel that had been spread over his groin and upper thighs. He reminded Dave of a fish, with his glowingly white potbelly and his gaping mouth, the red slash just above his hip, in the side of his stomach, as if his murderer meant to gut him like a crappie but had missed the mark. A butcher's knife was buried hilt-deep in his heart. Both of his knees were badly bruised and one of them was cut open, most likely from an impact and not the knife.

Dave studied him closer and realized he didn't know him. Although Capability was in the same county where he'd lived his whole life, the fish camp was across the lake from the Shady Grove side, cutting it off from most everyone so that the people here did most of their business in the next town over rather than driving around the lake to get to their own county seat.

"Who is this man?" Dave asked.

"Who are *you*?" One of the fishermen asked with some amount of defiance, stepping forward. Dave couldn't hardly blame him for asking, though, since he and Nina had barged in as if they owned the place. A hand-rolled cigarette hung from the man's bluish-pink lips. He was likely in his late fifties, his thumbs hooked into the pockets of his jeans, which were held up by suspenders over a long-sleeved madras shirt. Dave glanced around and saw that none of them were from Shady Grove or they would have certainly known who he was. He had been famous round these parts and now he was infamous after what he had done, his picture plastered on the front page of *The Shady Grove Sentinel* back when it all happened.

"I live across the lake, at the Marie," he said, using local parlance for the Marie Marina, which Rex had named for his late mother. "And this is my neighbor, Nina." Dave nodded to Nina, and all eyes went to her.

"Hidy, boys," she said, in that assured and comfortable way that only women raised around lots of men possess. "I work for the local paper."

"We heard the screams," Dave explained, "so we jumped in a boat and came on over."

"I'm Burgess Noble," the fisherman said, and offered his hand to Dave. A working man's hand, beefy and callused. Oil under his nails as if he had been repairing an engine. Dave looked him in the eye as they shook. There was something Dave didn't like about him, but he couldn't say just what yet. This man pointed to the little man beside him, who looked like most of the farmers Dave had known his whole life. Quiet, unassuming, his hair a whiff of dandelion fluff. "This here is Tom Jenkins."

"How do," Tom said quietly.

"He ran this fishing camp," Noble said, nodding toward the dead man. He was speaking to Dave as if he were a police officer and not just somebody that lived on a houseboat across the lake. People had always done that with Dave, though. It's why he had so easily become the mayor of his hometown. People trusted him without knowing why. "His name was Esau Campbell."

Dave recognized the name. The Campbells were the richest family in the whole county and Dave had heard talk of how Esau had always been a disappointment to them, not following in his politician father's footsteps. The Campbells not only owned more of the lakefront property than anybody else, but they also controlled it as Salem Campbell had served as the state representative for this district for as long as Dave could remember. Dave knew that Esau had a run-in with the law a few years back, although he couldn't remember exactly why, and that his father had set him up with this job, where his penchant for drinking and gambling in the evenings fit right in with most of the clientele.

"And who found him?" Nina asked.

"That Yankee-man over yonder found him and went into fits." Noble jabbed at the air with his thumb, pointing toward the short, round man sitting on the cinderblock wall near the path up to the cabins who was being comforted by a woman whose blond hair was covered in green plastic rollers. The poor guy was clearly traumatized, repeatedly rubbing his hands over his face as if to wipe away the image of what he had seen. "That's who you heard screaming."

"So Esau was running out of the shower house when he was killed?"

"No," Noble said, without further explanation.

Then Dave knew what it was about him that he didn't like: Noble had taken on the role of being in charge by his own election. That always had rubbed Dave the wrong way. For Dave, others naturally turned to him for leadership. But Dave predicted this guy always took charge whether others liked it or not. He had gathered from Noble's dialect and especially the spitting sort of way he had said "Yankee-man" that Noble was most likely from within the tri-county area, even if he wasn't a nearby local, and would probably have figured out who Dave was by now. *That mayor that got drunk and drove into the courthouse*, he'd tell his friends later. People always had a good laugh about that.

"So why was he *outside* the shower house, naked?" Dave asked. "Did he crawl out here?"

"Well, we brought him out here," Tom offered.

"Why'd you do a thing like that?" Dave said, too harshly. Even if he hadn't been a sheriff once upon a time *and* a lifelong reader of murder mysteries, he would have had enough sense to know a murdered corpse shouldn't be messed about with.

Apparently the fisherman knew this, too, because he looked embarrassed and deflated a bit. "I don't know. We panicked," Tom said. "Thought he might still be alive. And the electricity had been cut in the shower house. So me and Frank—we just picked him up under the arms before we even thought."

"Who is Frank?"

"He's staying here at the camp, too," Noble said. "He went to call the police."

Dave noticed that Nina had produced a reporter's notebook from somewhere and was furiously taking notes.

"So where is he now?" Dave said.

"No phone here at the camp," Noble explained. "Closest one is at the store up at the top of the hill. So he went up there. I imagine he'll be back directly."

Dave dotted his finger on the air as he counted. "So there were a total of six people at the camp when this happened, including Esau."

"Yep," Noble answered. "Me, Tom, the Yankee couple, and Frank White. He should be back any minute." This man seemed awfully intent on reminding Dave of that.

"Nobody saw anything?" Dave asked. They were all looking to him now, thinking he could help in this situation, so he had to get it sorted out. In this moment, he realized he had missed having that kind of purpose since he lost his job.

Noble and Tom told him no.

"I was sleeping like the dead," Tom said, then cringed at using such a phrase during this unfortunate event.

"I never heard a thing until the Yankee started screaming," Noble said.

"Does 'the Yankee' have a name?" Dave asked. The tension between the South and the North here didn't really have anything to do with the Civil War so much as it did the love-hate relationship with tourists. People in these parts tended to find the visitors from the North too demanding and nasally for their taste, always in a hurry to get things done even though they had come to the lake to supposedly relax. Dave understood the strain, but he didn't like the sneering way this man used the word "Yankee." He could easily hear him applying the same disgust to much worse words.

"Him and his wife haven't mixed any, so I don't know."

Dave knew time was of the essence in a case like this, so he wasn't about to wait for the sheriff and his dumb deputies to take over before he gathered some information. A man was dead, somebody needed to try to figure out how and why. So, like he had done all of his life, Dave went into action.

"I don't think you should go in there, Dave," Nina called from behind him as he made his way into the shower house. He ignored her. "All right then," he heard her say with derision as he went through the door.

Inside the windowless cinder block shower house was shadowy darkness. The fishermen who had carried out the body had left the shower running. The sound of the pounding water seemed loud within the concrete building. Dave ran his hand along the concrete walls until he found the breaker box on the wall in the space that would be behind the door when it was opened. One movement of his fingers and the overhead lights were back on.

At the front were two urinals and two commodes within narrow stalls. Just past those there were no stalls for the showers, simply four showerheads protruding from the back wall. The one second from the right was still running, and its sound seemed to grow louder in Dave's ears.

He could see no harm in turning off the water, but he let it run despite the fact that waste of this sort troubled him deeply. Still, he didn't want to compromise the crime scene in any way before the police got in there. Not that there would be much to find: the water splashing against the concrete floor had washed away any blood or other evidence. Clever place to kill someone in that regard.

Dave turned, doing a 360 to take in the entire scene. Then he saw that the entire wall by the entrance had been written across in blood:

SINS OF THE FATHER

Neat block letters, except where some of the blood had dripped down the wall.

Dave walked to the words as if in a trance. The closer he got, the more he was sure it was not blood, after all, but red paint.

The killer could have gotten away without a trace but had chosen to stop and leave this message written on the wall, had taken the chance of getting caught to say something to the world. So this wasn't just a murder. This person was out of their mind. Or just evil. Or someone who wanted people to know why this was happening. Maybe a little of all.

Dave reconstructed it in his mind: this fellow Esau had been caught up in his hot shower and the murderer had slipped into the room, eased open the breaker box, pulled down the switch to cut the electricity. The killer had dashed across to him before Esau had time to go into full panic, slashed the knife into Esau's side to gut him like a fish, then brought the knife up to drive it into his heart. Esau had fallen heavily onto his knees, maybe causing one or both of them to crack against the concrete, then he had fallen forward onto his face, allowing gravity to drive the knife farther in while the killer wrote his message on the wall and then disappeared into the night.

The likeliest scenario, although there could have been many ways it had all gone down. But what time had all this happened? Had Esau gone to shower last evening, before bed, and been lying there all the night before the tourist found him? Or had he risen early for the day at work and stumbled his way to refresh himself before anyone else got up? Had the man from Ohio only barely missed the whole grisly act?

"Dave, get out of there!" Nina called from the doorway. "The police are here!"

Dave took in every detail he could, but there wasn't much: the message, the wet concrete, the silver shower heads. If someone wanted to get away with murder, then this was the perfect crime scene.

Chapter 4

Once back outside, Dave found that dawn was easing itself out across the world. A yellow line of new sun showed itself over the eastern mountain. The mist was burning away against the farthest ridges, and the gathered people looked a more motley crew in the dim light of day. Both of the men—Noble and Tom—had five o'clock shadows growing all the way down their necks, ragged caps perched on their heads, ill-fitting pants and shirts. The other man—Frank, was it?—had returned from going to the store to summon the police and was leaning forward with a cigarette to a silver lighter that Noble had flicked open before him. This Frank was a handsome one with a headful of curly hair, a tight white T-shirt that showed off finely muscled arms, and a face like a movie star. Like that actor who hollered "Stella!" over and over in that movie, *A Streetcar Named Desire*, which Dave had liked but Janet had hated. Noble clicked the lighter shut, sucked hard on his own cigarette, and eyed Dave with suspicion.

The frightened man and his wife had disappeared, although Dave imagined the sheriff would pull them back out for questioning soon.

And—speak of the devil—there was the sheriff himself, climbing out of his black-and-white cruiser. Victor Burns had been Dave's best friend since their glory days playing basketball at Shady Grove High. They had even shipped out together and done basic training at Fort Campbell when they both volunteered on the same day. Dave was eventually sent to Germany and Victor to Egypt, but as soon as they returned home they took up where they had left off. They had done everything together. Dave and Victor were like brothers bonded by high school, the same small-town experience, and war, not to mention that the two men had pretty much run Shady Grove with Victor as the county sheriff and Dave as the town's mayor. Dave himself had been the sheriff for two years prior to winning the mayoral election. Victor was the only person Dave had ever trusted completely. He had trusted him even more than his own wife, and the men certainly got along better than he and Janet did. Janet never could be satisfied, no matter how hard Dave tried.

Janet had loved Victor's wife, Glory, and they became best friends, too. Neither couple had children—Dave and Janet because Janet had never wanted any, but Victor and Glory had both longed for kids. The two couples had done everything together: annual vacations to Gulf Shores, trips to Nashville for the occasional show at the Grand Ole Opry, Saturday grill-outs or Sunday dinners after attending services together at Shady Grove Methodist.

They were all happy when Glory became pregnant at the age of twenty-eight, just before it was deemed too late. Janet threw her an elaborate baby shower, but at the celebration Glory went into labor. They had thought so, at least. At first there was a joyful excitement as the women tried to comfort her. But then they saw the blood and enough of them were mothers to know that wasn't right. Glory was dead by the time they got her to the hospital. The baby didn't make it, either.

The months after were a blur for Dave. A whole year of blur. Looking back now, he thinks how he should have seen it all happening. But at the time they were all so caught up in the shock and grief and the taking care of Victor that he lost sight and logic of everything. He didn't notice a thing.

But then, he came home one day to find Victor and Janet in his very own kitchen, having a cup of coffee and waiting for him.

"What are you two up to?" Dave had said in a laughing voice as he entered the kitchen.

He should have known, as soon as he saw that neither of them had the courage to look at him when he came in.

Victor had held onto his coffee cup with both hands, staring down onto its surface. Janet sat at the table like a mannequin and looked past Dave, as if someone was standing right behind him.

"Has something happened?" Dave had asked.

After a time, Victor finally had the decency to look him in the eye. "Yes, buddy, something has happened, and I'm sorry. I never meant to hurt you."

"What do you mean?" Dave had said. He stood there in the middle of the yellow kitchen, knowing completely and also not knowing anything at all, totally confused. A silence stretched between them, pocked only by the *nit-nit-nit* of the plastic red clock hanging over the kitchenette.

Once Janet spoke up, he could have sworn there was a bit of pleasure in her voice. "What's happened is that Victor and I have fallen in love, Dave," she said as matter-of-factly as someone on the radio reading off tobacco prices for the week. There was certainly no regret in her voice or her posture. "We've fallen in love and we want to be together."

Dave would have grabbed Victor by the shirt collar and lifted him from the chair and thrown him through the kitchen window if Victor hadn't looked up at him with so much hurt on his face. He *was* sorry, and Dave could see it plain as day. But he had still gone through with it, hadn't he? He was only sorry that he'd had to tell his friend. He was only sorry that he couldn't have Dave's friendship and his wife, too.

A strange calmness had overtaken Dave.

"All I can tell you is good luck, Victor," he said. "You'll need it with her. If you can make her happy, you're a better damn man than me. And you're not a better man. You know that as well as I do."

"Now, listen, Dave," Victor had begun, "we can—"

"You can both go to hell," Dave had said, and left the door open behind him. When he got to his car and was about to back out of the driveway, he saw that Victor had come out onto the front porch, calling for him. He'd had the gall to come out onto Dave's own front porch. On

Dave's own house, like he owned the damn place now. Dave had the urge to bound from the car, run across the yard, and smash Victor's nose, then straddle him so he could beat on his head a while. But instead he pushed down on the clutch, notched the gearshift into first, and hit the gas, his two back tires each sending out little barks on the pavement.

Chapter 5

And here was Victor now, stepping out of his car and adjusting his pistol belt, a habit he had established long ago to draw people's attention to the fact that he had a gun and that he was in charge.

"Who can talk to me about what's happening here?" Victor said, scanning the crowd of fishermen who stood in a clump near the body. He hadn't seen Dave yet.

The fisherman named Noble took a step forward and started to speak, but Dave beat him to it.

"What happened is this man"—he pointed to the body—"was murdered in the shower house. The men here carried the body outside. The murderer left a message on the wall."

Victor looked more confused than surprised. "Dave, what are you doing here?"

"I can be anywhere I damn well please, I reckon."

Victor deflated a little. Dave hadn't seen him up close in the year since his marriage to Janet, and Dave could see that their life together had already taken a toll on Victor. The two of them had thought their grief could be eased if they were together, and it had obviously not worked.

Well, tough shit. He deserved it. They both deserved it.

"Come on, now, Dave. You know how this works," Victor said. "This is an active crime scene investigation and I can't have shenanigans going on here." Victor shoved his hands deep into his trouser pockets. "Why are you here?"

"We were at the Marie and heard screaming, so we came here to see if we could help," Nina said, stepping up beside Dave.

"And who are you, miss?" Victor asked.

"Well, I'm old enough to not be called miss," Nina said. Even as a child she had been good at making judgment calls. Dave could see that she didn't like Victor, not one bit. They hadn't known each other as children because Victor had moved to Shady Grove in high school, after her family had moved away.

"I'm sorry, ma'am," Victor said, sighing. "As the county sheriff I'm asking you who you are."

"I'm Nina Owens," she said, and held up her press pass. "I'm the new reporter for the *Sentinel*. And I'm an old friend of Dave's."

"A friend," Victor said, almost to himself. He was sizing up the two of them, Dave could tell. So he thought they were a couple. Good. Let him. Let him run tell Janet that Dave had a new woman. That'd burn her up. She was the kind of person who would prefer that her ex be miserable the rest of his life even if she was the one who had wanted out of the marriage.

"That's right," Nina said, all tough as nails. As a long-time small-town reporter, she had almost certainly had her fill of sheriffs who thought they ran everything. And she had almost certainly shot plenty of them down from their high perches.

"I'll need you all to clear the scene," Victor said, speaking up loud enough for the fishermen to hear, too. He looked around for his deputy, who was fumbling about, acting as if he was assessing the situation. "Please go on up to that first cottage and wait on the porch—"

"How long do you expect us to wait up there?" Noble asked while the others murmured to one another behind him. "I was supposed to go home today."

"We'll need to question each of you individually," Victor's deputy said, puffing up his chest. Dave recognized him as Zeke Collins and wondered how he had held onto his job as long as he had. He was about as smart as a box of hair. "You can plan on being here a while, mister."

Deputy Collins was carrying the crime scene equipment—toolbox, camera, more—from the trunk of the cruiser and lost his footing, his legs twisting over one another until he had nearly fallen, letting out a jagged cry.

"Collins, leave that to me," Victor said. "Jesus God," he said under his breath.

Up on the porch, the three men were laughing at the scene. Collins twirled to face them, ever the offended cop: "What are you bunch laughing at?"

This caused them to laugh harder.

"Looks like you have a crack team assembled, Victor," Dave said.

"I'm asking you again to clear the scene, Dave. I'm just trying to do my job."

"Kiss my ass, Victor," Dave said, and made his way for the porch. He knew Victor was right, but he had to get in as many hits against him as he could.

Dave might not like his former best friend much these days, but he knew Victor was a good police officer. He certainly had enough on his plate: Shawnee County had the lowest budget of any county in the state and no crime scene investigative team at all. Victor and his deputies, along with the county coroner, were the whole operation.

The fishermen talked in low voices as they clumped together on the cottage porch next to where Dave and Nina had taken seats on the wooden steps to watch Victor and Collins go about their "investigation," which involved a lot of Victor standing with his hands on his hips in long silence and Collins saying, "What're you thinking, boss?" several times.

The fishermen seemed to all be rough, hard-working men who had just wanted a little getaway. Frank, the only one Dave hadn't talked to yet, had a bluish-green coal tattoo—the tell-tale mark of someone who has been in a mining accident—on his cheek. Noble's hands showed that he worked with engines or at least with machinery; he was most likely a mechanic since the stain of oil never completely came out. Tom, the quiet one who now sat whittling with his pocketknife, struck Dave as a farmer. Farmers were the kind of men who could find a stillness for themselves without being still, just as Tom was doing right now with the piece of cedar in his left hand and the Case knife—blue as berries—in his right. The man certainly knew how to shoot a perfectly straight spear of tobacco juice through the small gap between his two front teeth.

"He probably tried to cheat somebody else out of money," the coal miner, Frank, said.

"I hope he didn't suffer too long," Tom offered, so low that Noble asked him to repeat himself. But when Tom looked up he saw that Dave was watching them, and listening to them, so he went silent.

Nina locked eyes with Dave and smiled, knowing that he was analyzing all of them just as she was.

"Somebody in his own family probably had him killed," Noble offered. "The Campbells ain't nothing but a bunch of crooks."

"I just want to get on back home. My wife needs me there," said Frank.

After a while Victor looked back toward the porch and nodded his head in a "Come here" gesture. He shifted his weight and hooked one thumb into his belt, a practiced gesture. Dave could imagine him trying out different postures in front of his hallway mirror, hoping to appear tough.

"You'll have to give more direction than that," Nina said. Then, to Dave: "Does he think we can read his mind as to which one of us he wants?"

"Dave. Can you come down here?"

Dave didn't want to do one damn thing that Victor asked him to. But he was at the scene of a murder.

He gave Nina a look of resignation and hopped from the steps then strolled down to where Victor stood near the body. A breeze drew the rich scent of the lake up to wash over his face, feeling like two handfuls of cold water against his skin. The sky was paling into a soft blue, promising a beautiful day that would pay no attention to the tragedy playing out inside it.

"Yes, sir?" Dave said, laying on as much sarcasm as possible.

"I'm going to ask you something and I hope you won't laugh in my face in front of everybody here."

"Victor, it's taking everything in me not to punch you in the face, much less laugh in it."

"If I could change things I would, Dave."

"Come on, Victor. Cut the bullshit."

"I didn't mean for things to happen the way they did. I would have never—"

"What do you want, Victor?" Dave planted his fists on his hips.

"I want you to let me deputize you. This is some serious business. Inside the shower house we've got a—"

"Message left by the murderer."

Victor heaved a sigh. "You went in there?"

"I had to make sure nobody else was hurt in there. I was here a good fifteen minutes before y'all."

"I need more help than Collins."

"No doubt. He's a dumbass."

Victor sighed. "He has some good qualities, too," he said. "The thing is, you're the only man around here who knows as much about the law as I do."

"I know more," Dave said.

"Well, yes, you most likely do," Victor said, not smiling. Just stating a fact. "That's why I need you. We haven't had a murder like this since—"

"The murders at Fogtown," Dave interrupted. He hadn't said the name of the place aloud in a long time and now he found a shiver crawling up his back. There was something off about Fogtown—something wrong with the entire place. He had witnessed real evil there, and he didn't like to think about it.

"Which you solved on your own when everybody else was stumped. And I can't remember ever having one where somebody did something as crazy as leave a message in blood."

"It's paint," Dave replied.

"Will you help me out?"

"What will the whole county think," he said, "deputizing the mayor who got drunk and ran his car into the courthouse?"

Victor was unfazed. He looked back at the crowd on the porch, who were all watching them with keen interest. "I think they'll be more concerned that a cold-blooded killer is on the loose. And you and I both know that you getting drunk and running your car into the courthouse made most people around here love you even more. You're the one who resigned."

Yesterday Dave could not have imagined even having a cordial exchange of hellos with Victor. Now he was seriously considering partnering up with him. But only because he knew he could be helpful.

"I need someone to help me with the questioning, Dave," Victor said, "and there's nobody better suited for something like this than you."

Victor didn't have to tell Dave what he was alluding to: back when Dave was sheriff, the worst murder to ever happen in Shawnee County had occurred, and Dave had figured out the whole thing on his own. Well, nearly on his own. He had almost been killed doing it, and the case had taken him to a place that made him believe in pure evil, but in the end it worked out. Some part of him had never gotten over the thrill of that chase and the satisfaction of putting that killer behind bars.

"We've got a crazy person on the loose," Victor said. He had always known just how to talk Dave into things, and now he homed in on Dave's love for this community. "We owe it to the county to do this right."

Dave nodded before he realized he was going to. "All right. But only because I care about this place. Not because I give a damn about helping you."

"Fair enough." Victor put his hand out so they could shake on it.

Dave puffed air between his lips in a show of ridicule. He wasn't about to shake Victor's damn hand. "We're not that far along yet."

Victor nodded. "All right. I'll get Collins to isolate the witnesses and keep an eye on them while you do the interviews."

"That'll work," Dave said. Before he turned to go Victor paused, opened his mouth to say more, but decided not to. Dave wasn't going to give him a break, so he stood before him with his hands on his hips, not taking his eyes from his old friend until finally Victor stalked away to find Collins.

Chapter 6

There was a shelter house with four picnic tables and a big grill down near the water's edge. This would do just fine as a questioning space. Dave told Victor that it made more sense to get everyone right here while it was all fresh instead of taking them down to the station, and Victor nodded and told him to line them up. He had Collins give Dave a yellow legal pad and a green pencil (SHAWNEE COUNTY SHERIFF'S OFFICE stamped in gold down its side) while he and Collins roped off the shower house and the body.

Frank seemed like the one most in a hurry to get out of there, so Dave had already decided to save him for last. Noble, on the other hand, was taking it all in, looking excited. Earlier he had acted like he was anxious to leave, but he seemed to enjoy watching all this play out. Nosey. Best to get the most inquisitive one off the crime scene soon, so Dave called him down first.

As soon as Noble sat down across from him, the older man fished his long fingers into the front pocket of his overalls and plucked out a pack of Pall Malls. He stuck one in his mouth, fired his silver Zippo, and sat back just as he released a great plume of smoke that shifted back over his head in the breeze.

Dave asked his name and residence.

"My full name's Burgess Noble," he said, and tapped the end of his middle finger to the point of his tongue, where a speck of tobacco rested, "and I live in Fogtown, Kentucky."

Dave started at hearing the name of the community again. Twice in one day. No use in asking for a phone number since Fogtown was so far out the telephone lines hadn't reached them yet.

"You've lived there since you returned from the war?"

"No. Grew up there. I worked on fishing boats up and down the Mississippi before and after the war. Just settled back there at my folks' place this January, after my dad passed away."

"I'm sorry for your loss," Dave said.

Noble looked at him with steely eyes, as if what Dave had said was more of an insult than a condolence. Or maybe as if he had drifted away somewhere for a moment, carried back in time on some old trauma. His wasn't the look of someone studying on a good memory, that's for sure.

"And you've been to the fishing camp before?"

"Oh yeah," Noble answered, snapping back. The day was already warming up and he unbuttoned the long sleeves of his cotton shirt and began rolling them up.

"How many?"

"This makes my third time," Noble said. "I came back in March for the trout. Last month walleye were biting good, and this trip I came for the bluegill. They're on the nest." He finished rolling up the sleeve of his right arm, revealing a tattoo of a square-shoulder thunderbird on his forearm. Dave knew what this meant.

"You were in the army," Dave said.

Noble nodded, nonchalant.

"Unit?"

"Seventh Army's Forty-Fifth Infantry."

"The unit that liberated Dachau."

"The very one," Noble said, and gave his cigarette a thoughtful inhalation. "But I was ordered to stay at base that day. Somebody's got to do it."

Lucky, Dave thought, but didn't say aloud. Although he would have offered the information in a normal conversation, Dave didn't think it was appropriate to tell the man he had been with the Third Army's Sixth Armored Division when they liberated Bergen-Belsen. Mostly Dave tried to forget everything about those days. The skeletal living bodies. The rotting dead bodies. The filth. The graves. The room completely full of shoes. He had picked one of them up. A red Mary Jane with a silver buckle that would have fit a girl of maybe four or five. He dreamt of that shoe sometimes. In his sleep he could feel it on his palm. Perhaps Noble was able to forget all he had seen for small spaces of time while he floated in a johnboat out on the still waters of Cedar Lake in the evenings, waiting for a bass to strike.

"And you knew the deceased pretty well, you'd say?" Dave asked.

"Naw, I wouldn't say that. We had played cards together a couple nights. Drunk some whiskey in the evening when we came in off the water. Not the kind of person you get to know."

"And y'all played cards last night."

"Sure did," Noble said. "Esau cleaned house. He took the haul last night."

"How much did he win?"

"A little more than a hundred, I believe. That's a lot for a fishing camp game."

"I'll say," Dave said, acting as if he had poker experience although he had always avoided gambling, even when he was in the service. "Was the poker game genial?"

"What do you mean by that?" Noble brought one leg up and rested his ankle atop his knee. Only then did Dave realize this leg was wooden. He could tell by the way Noble had hoisted it up in one quick motion and now, with the pants leg rising up, he could see the unnatural shine of the beige wood, painted to match his skin tone but failing terribly. A man like Noble would possess legs much whiter than his arms. Dave wondered if he had lost the leg in the war, which seemed the most likely cause.

"I mean did everyone get along and have a good time?"

"Oh yeah. A good bunch of boys down here this week. There were just the four of us playing. Me, Esau, Tom, and Frank."

"You know Tom and Frank, too?"

"No, I just met them this weekend. I've spent some time cleaning fish with Tom. He's a hell of a fisherman."

"And Frank?"

"We've all three been here two nights and we've played cards and done some drinking each night, so I feel like I know him a little. Card shark. Better at poker than he is at fishing. He hasn't caught a thing this whole trip." Noble laughed a little in a likable way. Dave could see he was the kind of man that grew on you. Gruff and suspicious at first, but easy to talk to once he warmed up. There was a charm there, buried, but charm could imply a good heart or one that wanted to disguise its rot. Some of the meanest people he'd ever known had also been among the most charming—his father, for one.

"But you said Esau took a big haul last night. So why do you call Frank the card shark?"

"Esau got lucky," Noble said. "That happens sometimes. But Frank has a strategy, and he's a cool player. He beat us all bad the first night."

"So it likely made him mad that Esau won last night."

"I wouldn't think so. It seemed like to me that Frank's too good a card player to get upset over losing once in a while to a lucky player." Noble patted his shirt pocket as if he had forgotten he put his cigarettes there. He lit another one, breathing out smoke with his words. "He wasn't a sore loser about it. I hate to play a sore loser worse than anything. Being a sore loser will get you killed quicker than winning."

Dave raised his eyebrows. "Why do you say that?"

Noble tugged down the hem of his pants' leg. When that didn't cover his wooden leg properly, he pulled up his white sock. "Just a saying. Nobody likes to play with a sore loser. That's no fun."

"Everybody thought Esau won fair and square?"

"Sure did," Noble said. "Far as I know."

"You said Frank hadn't caught any fish in the two days he's been here," Dave said, zeroing in on something interesting. "Do you all go out together?"

"I went out with Tom every day. Normally I have my own boat but when I got ready to leave home, my engine wouldn't fire up. I didn't want to cancel my trip, so I figured I'd just rent a boat from the camp. But once I met Tom he offered for me to go with him, so I did. He's got a 50 Evinrude on it, so that little thing just zips you across the lake."

"But Frank. He goes out alone?"

"Yep."

"Do you know where he goes?"

"Not my job to keep up with him," Noble said, and although the phrase was that of a smart aleck, Dave chalked this up more as the man's general personality instead of taking it personally.

"But you're sure Frank has been going out fishing?"

Noble nodded then carelessly flicked his ashes onto the floor of the shelter house. "He's gone out on the lake every morning. He rented his boat from the camp. He heads toward Tennessee, but Tom and I both fish in Kentucky," Noble said, referring to the way the lake straddled the state line.

Dave next asked Noble to tell him about what they first saw when they went into the shower house, but he added nothing Dave hadn't figured out on his own, especially since Noble had been in there in the dark and hadn't even seen the message on the wall.

"Do you have any idea when Esau went to take a shower?"

Noble laughed in the back of his throat, dislodging some phlegm that caused him to have a little coughing fit. When he had recovered he said, "Now why in the world would I know that?"

Dave didn't crack a smile. "Maybe he said he was going to shower when you all parted ways after the poker game. Maybe you saw him going in there."

"I have no idea when he went to take a bath. Last time I saw him was when we all left his cabin about half past two this morning."

"Was the poker game in his cabin both nights?"

Noble nodded.

"Would you say he was sober, drunk, or somewhere in between when you left?"

"I didn't know the man but if I was betting, I'd say Esau was a drunk, mister. But a drunk who is always functioning. You know what that's like."

Unfortunately, he did. Dave had lived with a father like that his entire childhood.

Dave told Noble that he could go on home but to call the sheriff's office if he thought of anything else.

Noble rose slowly, as if his back was giving him trouble, but once he had stood he paused there, silent, as if there were words he couldn't quite get formed.

"Is there something else you need to say?" Dave asked.

"There's many a person who probably wanted to kill ole Esau, but it wasn't any of us here at the camp."

"Why would many people want to kill him?" Just as Dave said this, he could see Nina sprinting across the hill, calling out to Victor as if something was wrong, but he had Noble talking good, so he couldn't interrupt him now.

"Because he was a mean little banty rooster."

"I thought you liked him."

"He was good company for whiskey and cards. For a couple hours. But past that and he got obnoxious. Either crying about how bad his family did him or talking big talk. No matter what, just knowing him a couple nights I could tell he had to always have the best story. He always had to outdo everybody else." Noble looked hard into Dave's eyes. "You know the only thing worse than a sore loser? A sore winner. Last night he was laughing, rubbing it in Frank's face that he had won."

"That didn't bother Frank?"

"I don't think so. He just laughed about it. I would've probably knocked the hell out of him."

Down the hill behind Noble, Victor was making his way to the shelter house, a pained look on his face. Noble saw that Dave was distracted, so he turned to see what was happening.

"Thanks for your cooperation, Mr. Noble," Dave said. Noble faced him and Dave put out his hand. The man shook it weakly. "I'll be in touch if we have any follow-up questions."

And just then, Victor reached them. Dave knew Victor well enough to know—without him even speaking—that they had a new problem on their hands.

Chapter 7

Frank had eased to his car without anyone noticing—even though Collins had been told to keep an eye on the witnesses—and would have slipped away completely unnoticed if Nina hadn't been perched on one of the cabin's porches working up her story in her notebook. Dave had thought right away that the proper thing for Victor would have been to get the press as far away from this crime scene as possible, but he wasn't about to intervene in matters that would exclusively help Victor.

"I've radioed in for backup from the boys in Burkesville and Byrdstown. Zeke is in pursuit, but Frank got a good five-minute lead on him, and all these old country roads back in here—he could've gone one of three dozen different ways," Victor said. He was talking to Dave like nothing had ever happened, like he hadn't made a cuckold of him in front of the whole county, like a light switch had been flicked making everything go back to normal. Victor had known him since they were teenagers, so he saw this thought playing out on Dave's face. "You're my deputy now, so I'm talking to you like one."

Dave felt heat rise to his face and he clenched his right hand into a fist. "I'm *a* deputy. For Shawnee County. Not *your* damn deputy," Dave spat. If he wasn't so curious about all this, he would have walked away right then.

"I get it, all right?" There was nothing but deference in Victor's voice. He was in a hard spot and he knew it. For a second, Dave wondered if Victor was giving him this chance because he knew how much Dave loved investigations and because he had nothing else in his life to occupy him right now. But no, Victor was only looking out for himself and Dave was the best person to help him out. Dave couldn't see him as anything but self-centered after what he had snuck around and done with Janet.

"And I appreciate your help," Victor was saying. "I called KBI, and they just want updates. They're not sending anybody in. It's just us, so I need all the help I can get."

It would have certainly helped to have more resources, but often the boys from the Kentucky Bureau of Investigation were more hindrance than help. They had better equipment, but their minds weren't any better than the locals. They liked to make a big show of their lab work and all, but ultimately cases like this boiled down to old-fashioned detective work. Figuring it out.

"I found his address in the camp roster and I radioed for the state troopers to go there, so they'll most likely be waiting if he arrives at his house," Victor said.

That reminded him. Dave had an inkling of why Frank had skedaddled. "Have you searched Esau's cabin yet?"

"I'm still mapping out the shower house," Victor said, squinting against the sun shining off the water a few yards away. Nearing nine o'clock, and already the day was heating up. Too beautiful a day for a murder investigation, for sure.

"We need to check it out," Dave said. "Right now."

Nina had gone back to her post on the porch and was bent over her notebook, scribbling away furiously. Victor caught sight of Dave glancing up at her and finally realized what Dave had thought an hour ago.

"I can't have the press here while this is going on, Dave. You want to tell her to head out, or should I?"

"Are you kidding me?" Dave sneered. "If you want me on board you are *always* going to play the bad cop and I'm always going to be the good one. Got it?"

Victor put both hands on his belt and turned.

"Tell her to take Rex's boat back and I'll get a ride over when I'm done here," Dave called, and Victor raised a hand but didn't turn back to face him as he walked away.

Up on the porch, Nina put a hand to her brow, looking down and most likely figuring out that she was about to be booted.

★ ★ ★

Esau Campbell's cabin was the den of someone who didn't have much of a life. Spartan, with only the necessities in each room. The place was surprisingly neat; Dave had expected a dingy mess. But in the small front room everything seemed to have its place. A rain jacket on a hook near the front door, a record player and radio on a table near a threadbare couch. In the wire rack on the bottom of the table there were albums by Red Foley, Ernest Tubb, Tex Ritter, and The Carter Family. He had good taste, at least. There was a wingback chair that looked like it had once been expensive but was now a hand-me-down and a bookcase devoid of any reading material besides three worn Louis L'Amour Westerns and a Bible that made a crack when opened to suggest it had never been looked at before. The pages stuck together enough to prove Dave's initial suspicion was correct. Instead, the shelves were full of small tackle boxes; a phone book (which was strange as there was no phone in sight); two framed pictures of a little boy with enormous freckles sprinkling the bridge of his nose and cheeks; and a poinsettia-decorated Christmas tin full of buttons, sewing thread, and needles.

The cabin was obviously a bachelor's pad, with no decor of any kind on the walls except for one framed photograph of the fishing camp from fifteen years ago when the lake had first been filled properly and the camp had just opened. Along the bottom in white print was etched: *Capability Fishing Camp, Cedar Lake, August 1 1940*. There were four more cabins in the picture than were currently here and what looked to be a nice general store in the photograph. There were tin signs on the front of the store advertising Sunbeam Bread and RC Cola, as well as a long bench where two men were laughing together. What could have happened to these buildings?

There was something else off, too, but it took Dave a few minutes to put it together. The boat ramp was in a different place now than in this picture. At some point a blacktopped road had been poured down to the dock where the present-day ramp was more conveniently placed than the one in the photograph.

Further proof of Esau's bachelorhood was the array of fish tackle, needle-nose pliers, spools of fishing line, and several small boxes of different-sized hooks on the coffee table. Still, they had been set out with precision, as if Esau had been working on his baits but always took time to line them up in symmetrical rows.

On the floor beside the coffee table stood a large silver kettle, which made no sense to Dave until he looked up and saw the light brown splotch on the ceiling that revealed a recent leak.

Dave strolled into the kitchen and found proof that a poker game had happened there last night. Esau had not cleaned up after the men left. There were three overflowing ashtrays, several empty brown Stroh's beer bottles, cracked peanut shells on the floor. There was also a half-empty bottle of Old Fitzgerald bourbon with the cap missing and three shot glasses near it. Yet there had been four players. He'd have to find out who had abstained, and why. The cards, however, had been put back into their packet and situated in the center of the table.

Dave pawed around in the garbage can but found only an apple core, a scattering of coffee grounds, and a brown paper sack stained with grease that suggested it may have held potato chips from the store up the hill. Certainly nothing worth bagging for evidence. A plate, glass, knife, and fork were standing shining in the dish drainer, which somehow struck Dave as sad. Maybe because it reminded him of his own lonesomeness. As much as he was relishing being a single man living on a houseboat without much to worry about, there were long nights when his watch ticked too loudly. More than once he had washed his own single plate, glass, knife, and fork and wondered what life was for if you didn't have anyone to share it with. Half a minute later he'd be thinking how people weren't worth the effort, how they'd always let you down, how you were better to just fend for yourself and let it be. But still, there was that nagging lonesome feeling that threatened to turn into the full-on blues. There was something even more depressing about finding this in common with a dead man.

He couldn't help hearing Jelly Roll Morton's jaunty piano playing one of his favorite tunes, "Dead Man Blues," but when he almost started humming the song, it felt far too maudlin.

He refocused on the scene to shake these thoughts from his mind.

The sink was empty, but the drawer for the cutlery had been left fully open, with all the forks, spoons, and butter knives pushed around in disarray. Below it, the only other drawer in the kitchen held dishtowels and had been shoved shut so hastily that it had gone off its tracks inside the cabinet.

In the bedroom he found exactly what he had expected: it had clearly been ransacked. The mattress off-center so it appeared to have been searched under and then dropped quickly. A chifforobe stood open with three of its drawers left pulled out and one thrown onto the floor. A nightstand had been opened so hastily that the lamp that had most likely stood there had fallen over and broken. The shelf under the nightstand was empty, which made Dave wonder if a pistol normally lived there. That's where Dave kept his in case he needed it quickly, and most men he knew did the same. The top shelf of the closet was empty, and Dave suspected the winter clothes that now lay in the bottom of the closest had originally rested there before a searching hand had tossed them onto the floor.

The question was, had Esau's murderer burgled the place after he killed Esau? Or had Frank gone in there after the murder to find the money he had lost to Esau last night and claim it for his own?

Or was Frank the murderer?

Chapter 8

As soon as Dave stepped out onto Esau's small porch, he saw the couple from up North climbing the hill toward him. The old farmer, Tom, was waiting patiently on his own cottage porch, whittling on a short branch.

The woman was stomping along in a fury while her husband struggled to keep up behind her. She seemed to have modeled her whole look on Marilyn Monroe. Her hair had been dyed so blond that it looked more like white cotton candy. Her lips and nails had been painted to match in a stark red. She had positioned a tiny black beauty mark on her cheek and the top three buttons of her blouse had not been latched, allowing a peek at the delicate lace of her brassiere. There were small red cherries all over her dress, which fit like a movie star's, too, accentuating her curves. The woman clenched a red purse in her hand and of course her red sandals revealed toenails that had been carefully polished to match her fingernails. All this red—the cherries, the purse, the nails, the lips—struck Dave as inappropriate for a place where so much blood had so recently been spilled, but he reckoned the woman couldn't help what she had packed far in advance. There was a strange mix of elegance and roughness about her. The elegance mostly rested in her shape while her movements revealed her as someone who had been raised in the country, someone who did everything in a big, determined way. He could easily see her rushing around a farm to milk a cow, muck out the pig sty, and toss hay over her shoulder with a pitchfork.

Her husband, on the other hand, was about the least interesting person Dave had ever seen. Plain as a paper bag. A head shorter than his wife, balding, wearing a white button-up shirt and loose brown dungarees with penny loafers, a strange choice for shoes at a fishing camp.

"Hey, mister, are you about to interview us or not?" the lady called to him in a piercing Northern accent, stopping halfway up the hill as if she was not about to go any farther, and planting a fist on her hip. Her husband stopped behind her but seemed to cower in her shadow as if he was embarrassed his wife was being so forward with someone in charge.

Dave shuffled down the steps quickly. "Yes, I'm sorry to keep you waiting." He extended his hand as he neared them. "What were your names?"

She put out her hand first, inserting it into his palm with firm assuredness, like someone shaking his hand after a business deal has been struck. "I'm Denise Rose," she said, not impolite, but also letting him know she meant business and didn't have time for niceties. Her eyes were large, brown, and doe-like.

When Dave let go of her hand, she wiped it on her right hip as if his fingers had been clammy, although he knew they weren't. He took a step down the hill and was surprised by the strength of her husband's handshake, which pulled Dave toward him in the process, nearly knocking him off balance. "Ronald Rose," he said sheepishly, his tone in contrast to the confidence of his handshake. Perhaps ashamed by how upset he had been earlier.

"I'm Dave Hendricks, and I'm working as a deputy on this case." Dave stepped past them and didn't look back, expecting they'd follow even before he announced: "Let's go down to the shelter house where we can be comfortable."

As they went down the hill, he could see a boat streaking across the lake with two skiers behind it. A breeze eased in off the water and smelled of all the trees, lush with the green of high summer, and the rocky banks where the water washed up. Such a beautiful day, and he was stuck here. He should have been out on the water himself, anchored up in some shady cove catching bluegills that he'd fry up for supper, or having beers at a swimming hole with his friends. That had been the plan when he moved down here. To enjoy the lake every minute he could while he ate up his savings and tried to figure out what he'd do next with his life. He worked on the dock for Rex in exchange for the space for his houseboat, and he found that kind of manual labor pleasing: scrubbing boats, tending to the bait, playing handyman on the rentals.

But the bigger part of him loved the mystery, the interviewing, looking for evidence, the math of trying to figure it all out. Even if he had to work alongside Victor, he was happy to be involved. He had forgotten how good it felt to work on a case like this during his brief time as sheriff. He had slipped into the safe life of being Janet's husband, of being the mayor who had to smile and be polite to every asshole in town just so they'd keep supporting him. He had lost his edge, his curiosity. And now he felt it coming back to him.

Halfway to the shelter house, he realized the woman had been talking to him and he hadn't heard a thing she'd said.

"I'm sorry, Mrs. Rose, what was that?" he said, turning to her as he kept walking.

"I said, I hope we can make this quick because we have to be getting to Alabama. We were supposed to leave at six thirty this morning."

"We'll get you on the road as soon as possible, ma'am," he said, and sat down at the picnic table. "I'm sorry I can't offer y'all any coffee or anything—"

"That's kind of you, Deputy, but let's get on with it, and call me Denise, please," she said, carefully crossing her very nice legs and not bothering to tug down her dress over her knee. She sat straight-backed in her chair, on the edge of her seat, as if she were balancing a book on her head. Her husband sat with his hands folded in his lap and his eyes cast down, like a child who had recently been scolded. "We have a tournament waiting for us in Muscle Shoals," she said.

"Oh, you're a tournament fisherman, Mr. Rose?"

Ronald Rose looked up quickly, like a student who has drifted off in class and heard his name called. His mouth flew open but he didn't have time to respond before his wife threw back her head and laughed.

"No, I am," she said. "I hold the world record for the black crappie."

Well, Dave wasn't expecting a professional fisherwoman to be outfitted in a pretty cherry dress, but that's what he got for assuming anything. Everything had changed after the war.

"I'm sorry, ma'am, it was stupid of me to—" Dave said, then interrupted himself, stuttering: "W-wow, that is really something."

She gave a brisk nod and squared her shoulders. "Caught it over at Cherokee Lake, June of forty-nine. Four pounds, six ounces," she said, her mouth set firmly.

"That is a lot of meat on a crappie."

"Well, we didn't eat it, mister—I've forgotten your name."

"Dave Hendricks, ma'am—"

"Yes, that's right. We didn't eat it, Mr. Hendricks. We mounted it. With the others."

"Congratulations. And really, I'm sorry for—"

"People always assume my husband is the fisher, but I couldn't do it without him. He's quit his job to take care of me on the road. We go all over the world now to tournaments and conferences." At this she reached across and capped her hand over her husband's knee. "A lot of men are so small they protest a woman being in the tournaments. Many of the tournaments won't even let me in. I had to go to court to sue to get in the Cherokee Lake one. You can imagine how miffed they were when I pulled in that huge, fighting crappie!" Again she threw back her head and laughed, but her lips did not hold a smile once the laugh had escaped her. Her face went stony again. "But my husband has enough confidence to be with a strong woman. Most men can't do that."

Dave nodded emphatically, unconsciously mimicking her husband, who was doing the same while he looked at his movie-star-gorgeous-fishing-champion wife with admiration. This was an odd pair. The husband, full of deference but offering his wife exactly what she needed, the wife dressed like someone who might never touch a fish, much less pull in world records. But that's what was endlessly fascinating about human beings, Dave thought: we can never assume to know anything about any of them.

"She's aiming for the world record smallmouth, and this part of the world is bursting with them," Ronald said, his voice calming and even. Dave knew this fact well enough. The next lake over, Dale Hollow, held the world record for that already.

"Let's get started then, Mr. Hendricks," Denise said.

He wanted to remind her that she was the one who was slowing things down by sharing her adventures with him of her own free will, but he didn't.

"All right then, I just have a few questions."

"We didn't mix with any of those people," Denise launched in with a bored tone, as if she knew every question he would ask and had prepared her answers well in advance. "We got here two days ago, went out for a five-hour fishing trip both afternoons. I have a tournament here in two months and wanted to get the lay of the land more than anything else. Learn the bends of the lake. We got in around dusk, kept to our own cabin where Ronald fried us steaks and baked us potatoes both nights. Didn't speak to any of them."

"But you must have talked to Esau—um, to Mr. Campbell—"

"Only when we signed in and he gave us the key to our cabin," Denise answered. "We got here late that first evening, and I felt like he was in a rush to get us settled so he could get onto something more important."

"Why do you say that?"

"The whole time we talked to him, he looked over my shoulder, like he was expecting a car to pull down into the camp. He was preoccupied, fidgety."

"And you never heard or saw anything that might be helpful?"

Denise shook her head and looked at Ronald as if about to goad him into sharing some information. Before she had to, he spoke.

"Only one thing. The first night we were here, I couldn't sleep and went out onto our porch to smoke. I saw Noble and that other fellow he's always with go into their cabins. I figured they'd all been drinking together down at the camp manager's cabin."

"They played poker down there the last several nights."

"Must've been when the game closed up." This man spoke slowly, as if thinking over each word before he let it loose onto the air, so Dave was never quite sure if he was finished speaking or not.

Denise glanced at the dainty silver watch on her wrist. "Tell him the rest, Ronald."

"But then I saw the camp manager come out with that other one, the one that peeled out in his car a few minutes ago."

"Frank."

"I guess so, yeah."

"And did something in particular happen between them?"

"They were arguing. I couldn't hear what they were saying, but the one who left—Frank—he was giving the camp manager a mouthful. Telling him what-for."

"Did they get violent at all?"

"No, but they were plenty mad. Frank stomped off, and the camp manager told him he could go to hell."

"But this would have been the night before last," Dave said.

"That's right," Denise affirmed.

"The night before the night he was killed, then."

The couple nodded in unison, Denise's blond curls trembling around her face.

"This is good to know, Mr. Rose," Dave said. He was writing in his notebook as he spoke: *argument, not physical, go to hell*. "Before we get to you going to the shower house, I wonder if there's anything else you might think is important?"

Denise sighed, as if there was something she wanted to say but dreaded getting into it. She was giving him enough of a sign for Dave to say, "Ma'am?"

"The first full day we were here, I had Mr. Campbell put up a No Entry sign at the shower house so I could use it, and he offered to stand guard at the door while I was in there," she said, looking down at the lake. Her eyes were so trained on something that Dave turned, briefly, to see what she was staring at. Only the wide water. "They're not used to women being here, you see, so there is only the one space for bathing. Only a commode and sink in these cabins."

"That's antiquated," Dave said, although he figured this was probably the norm.

"Well, it should be, but most of these fishing camps have regulations that don't allow women to stay even if they're there with their husbands who are fishers," Denise said. Beside her Ronald lit a cigarette, waved out the match, then flicked it through the air so it pinwheeled to the ground. "But the thing is, when I came out of the shower house, that man, Frank, was standing there, talking to Mr. Campbell. I didn't know their names, but I'm calling him what you've said he's called."

"And were they arguing then?"

"No," she said slowly, as if confused by the question.

"You said 'the first full day' you were here. So that would have been the day after your husband saw them arguing."

"Yes," she said, but somehow she seemed unsure. "That's right. They looked thick as thieves to me. Standing close and whispering. I couldn't help feeling like they were talking about me. The way they looked at me when I came out. A woman just knows, you see. So I gave them a look to kill and strutted on by them. When I got a few yards away, I heard Campbell say, 'Snooty bitch.' I started to turn and give the both of them a piece of my mind, but I didn't. I didn't want to give them the satisfaction of my response."

"You never told me this!" Ronald said, and jumped from his chair. His demeanor before had been so calm that the raising of his voice seemed particularly forceful. Now he looked like the living embodiment of a gasket about to blow.

"I didn't want to get you riled up," she said, and reached out to take his hand in hers, which seemed to immediately calm him. Then, to Dave: "Ronald can get into such a rage about men being fresh with me, and it happens quite often, I'm afraid. The nature of being around fishermen a lot, I suppose."

Dave had no trouble believing any of this as Ronald's face had gone a deep red although she had cajoled him into sitting back down. If Dave was betting, he'd put his money on this being a great couple, a true love. He envied them that. Odd couples are often the best couples of all.

"But that's the last I saw of any of this lot until this morning when Ronald found the body," Denise said, and glanced at her watch again.

"Let's talk about that," Dave said, looking at Ronald. "I know you found the body inside the shower house, and I understand it was quite a scare for you."

"When I was eleven, I found my mother in a similar situation," Ronald said, his eyes on the floor. Then he looked up at Dave. "She had been murdered. Stabbed."

Denise reached over and took her husband's hand, running her thumb over his knuckles, causing him to flinch.

"Made it all worse that my father had killed her. He ran off, but they caught him—"

Sins of the Father, Dave saw spelled out on the air behind Ronald's head.

"And he died in prison a year later when his cellmate strangled him to death." Ronald seemed to grow larger before Dave's eyes, his entire posture changing so it seemed to even change the shape of his face, making him square-jawed where there had only a moment before been nothing but roundness. "It brought it all back, see. So that's why I couldn't stop screaming. It's embarrassing as hell, but it took me back to when I was a boy and—" Ronald put a hand to his mouth and looked down, trying to hide the tears that had come into his eyes.

"No wonder you were upset, Mr. Rose," Dave said. *Oh, all the ways that parents have harmed their children over the years.* He was still figuring out all the ways his own father had damaged him. "It's nothing to be ashamed of."

Then the man told him everything, but it wasn't much: he'd had a flashlight with him to see on the path from the cabin or he likely would have never seen the corpse and would've gone to bed without a shower. But he'd had the light with him and then he had started screaming and couldn't seem to stop, as if all the horror from all those years ago had been trapped, waiting for this moment to come out.

His wife was a whole different person now than she had been when they walked in here. By the time Ronald finished with his story, he had gained some new kind of confidence and his wife had lost some of hers. She leaned against him as they walked back up the hill toward their waiting car after Dave told them he'd be in touch if they needed anything else. He had nothing that would allow him to hold them. They'd definitely need to check out Ronald's mother's murder from thirty years ago, though. Dave had studied these two people for the last half hour and had seen many facets of them, but if there was one thing he knew for sure, it's that human beings were endlessly full of secrets.

CHAPTER 9

Dave had known the coroner, Vashti Bryant, since before he could remember. They had grown up just down the road from each other and had often played together with the rest of the kids that lived nearby. The town of Shady Grove was segregated, but out in the hills of Shawnee County the divisions were more about class: who was poor and who was well-off divided people out there. Neither Vashti's nor Dave's families had had any money.

At that age he hadn't given much thought to how Vashti wasn't allowed to go to the same school, how his father never mixed with her parents. That gulf widened as they got older. Vashti's favorite game as a child had been Funeral, so it was no surprise to any of them that she had run for coroner as soon as she came back from graduating top of her class at Kentucky State. The big surprise was that the people of Shawnee County had elected not only a woman but also a black woman. She had held the office ever since, and as a result she held a higher office than any other black woman in the state. She was the one who had called the game Funeral, but Autopsy would have been more accurate.

She and their friends had not pretended to bury someone; for them, Funeral was assisting Vashti while she examined the dead: a bluebird, beautiful even in death; a squirrel they found among the leaves; a spider that had drowned; a minnow found floating in the creek. The rest of them—Dave included—had always grown bored with the game quickly and would run away to play hide-and-seek or tag while Vashti remained bent over the dead, mumbling to herself about how the bird showed signs of having flown into a window or pronouncing the squirrel expired by way of heart attack while he was gathering acorns. Vashti had always been completely her own person. She was stubbornly single and devoted only to her job. She had never told him as much, but Dave figured she had her eye set on becoming the state medical examiner someday.

Vashti was bent over the body in deep concentration when Dave made his way back up the hill to her. The coroner's ambulance was parked just beyond her, with two young men leaning against it, smoking while they waited to take away the body. Dave had to speak her name twice to break the spell that had befallen her, and once she heard him, she put a finger up and wrote furiously on her clipboard before turning her face up to him. Her bright smile spread her mouth wide when she saw it was Dave.

"What are you doing here?"

He explained how he had ended up deputized.

"You, working for Victor? Yeah, *that* won't end in disaster," she said.

"Working for the people of Shawnee County, not for him," he said, but she was so pleasing that he couldn't get miffed at her. "I forgot how much I missed it."

"I always thought it was crazy when you left the real work and became a mayor," she said, smiling. Then her brow furrowed. "I should've called you after everything that happened," she said, meaning the divorce, his drunk driving, his humiliation—things so awful even Vashti wouldn't name them. "I didn't know what to say, but if it's any consolation, I'm glad you got away from Janet."

"You never did like her," he said.

Vashti kept her eyes on her work, but she had never minced words and wasn't about to now. "No, I didn't," she said.

Due to segregation they had gone to separate high schools, so she and Janet hadn't really known one another until they were all adults. At the few political functions they were all forced to attend together, she had avoided speaking to Janet unless she had to. In fairness, Vashti had never really liked many people, period. Now that he was older and wiser, this was one of the things Dave liked most about her.

"I still can't get over Victor betraying you," she said. "Everyone always knew he worshipped you. I wouldn't blame you if you were furious at him—"

"Well, I am—"

"But my money is on it being Janet's fault."

"Takes two to tango," Dave offered.

Vashti put her large eyes on his. Lord, she was gorgeous. He had thought that from the time they were teenagers, but by then Janet had already mesmerized him. "How do you like living down at the Marie?" Vashti asked.

"Houseboat living is the life for me. Come down sometime and have a whiskey on my back porch. Nice to watch the moon come up over the water."

She hesitated as if she didn't know quite how he meant this, but seemed to decide that didn't matter. "I might just do that," she said, and turned back to her work.

★ ★ ★

Dave's interview with the farmer, Tom, didn't tell him much more than what he had garnered from the Roses and Noble. Tom lived a couple of hours away in Cookeville, Tennessee. He was a widower who usually came here with his son, but this weekend he had come alone because some friends had said the fish were biting especially well. He was in his late seventies, he said, but he looked younger. His skin was a leathery brown from a lifetime of working out in the fields but his face was virtually unlined, perhaps because he had always worn a straw fedora, just as he was now.

Tom had no knowledge of Esau having owned a gun—"I barely knew the feller," Tom had said quietly—and he hadn't witnessed anything worth telling. No arguments between Esau and Frank or anyone else. Nothing unusual at the poker game.

"There were four of you but only three shot glasses. Do you remember who didn't drink?"

"Oh, I've not had a drink of nary thing in many a year, mister. Drinking caused me nothing but grief, so I quit it."

There was one curious thing that Tom remembered: he had seen two visitors come to Esau's cottage on Friday, one in the morning and one around dusk.

"Both of them parked up the hill and walked down," Tom said, his eyes on the piece of cedar he was whittling. Dave thought it best to not ask him to put it away; if he knew anything about old farmers like this, whittling was more of a centering thing than a distraction. "That evening we's cleaning fish down at the dock, and all I could tell is that it was a man who come to see him."

"A tall man? Or short?"

"More tall than average, I'd venture."

"Big, or—"

"Naw, slender," Tom said.

"Could you tell anything else about him? His face, for instance?"

Tom paused for a moment, the blade of his Case pocketknife silver and sharp as it rested against the wood. "I couldn't tell a thing about him," he said at last, looking up briefly. Then he drew the knife down the branch's side again.

"It was all of you cleaning fish: you, Noble, Frank, the Roses?"

"No, the Roses didn't mix with us," Tom said, looking Dave in the eye for a moment. "I don't believe they cleaned their fish, anyway. I never saw them do it."

"And the other visitor. They came that morning?"

"Yessir," Tom said, "Friday morning. Early."

"Before daylight early?"

"Nawsir, maybe an hour after daylight. I slept in that day. I never sleep in at home. But I was just getting up and I heard the car."

Dave wondered why the Roses nor Noble had not mentioned any visitors. Noble's cottage was even closer to the thin strip of road that served as a drive into the fishing camp, so he certainly should have heard a vehicle if he was awake.

"You didn't look out to see the car?"

"I've never been a particularly nosey feller," Tom offered.

"You never saw anyone else coming and going?"

"Well, Noble went to the store a couple hours later."

"Why? Do you know?"

"Got us some baloney, light bread, and mustard. We made sandwiches while we were out fishing. He offered to, since I had let him go out on my boat with me." Tom seemed to be finished with his whittling now. He wiped the blade of his pocketknife on the denim covering his thigh, closed the knife carefully and held it between the thumb and forefinger of his right hand. He laid the smooth piece of wood on the table. Its rich musky scent rose up between them. He looked out at the lake. "The lake is real pretty," he said, pronouncing it *purdy*. "But when I was a young man, before the lake, this was the prettiest country you ever seen in your life. Nowhere else could rival it. The prettiest rivers. Especially at the confluence, which I believe was right out yonder." He raised a crooked finger, most likely broken in some farming accident years ago, and pointed toward the big water between the marina and the fishing camp.

"Yes, it was," Dave said. "The confluence. I've been told that's right."

"You don't remember it?"

"I was raised a little farther upriver," Dave said. "My family never came down this way back then, before the lake."

"That's a shame," Tom said, and Dave could have sworn there was a deep sadness in the man's cornflower blue eyes. "My first wife and me, we used to picnic at the confluence. There was a little falls there and there was always a nice breeze. I don't know if it come out of the mountain or the falls. Our young'uns loved to wade there. I hate that it is gone forever. It was a thousand wonders, how pretty it was."

Dave had heard people talk about the confluence of the three rivers before but he had never heard it described quite as well, somehow. Dave realized then that this old man was lonesome. He wanted to chat. But there was still much to do.

"I'm sure it was, sir," Dave said, and stood, hand out. Tom shook it, giving his fingers a hard squeeze.

"That's all, then?" the old man asked.

"I believe so, Mr. Jenkins. If we need anything else from you, somebody from the sheriff's department will be in touch."

Tom stood, slid his knife into his pocket. Dave watched the old farmer as he struggled back up the hill and climbed into his truck. Once there he looked back and locked eyes with Dave, then nodded his head, and pulled away.

★ ★ ★

Dave found Victor's clipboard on the porch of the cottage nearest the shelter house, but didn't see the sheriff anywhere about. Dave looked over what all Victor had done and found that, as always, he was a professional. He had done everything he was supposed to.

He had measured the shower house (twenty feet by forty feet) and sketched a floorplan of the murder scene—not much work since the building was just one big rectangle with the urinals and toilets near the door and the shower spigots in the back wall.

The sheriff had lifted several fingerprints from the door, the breaker box, and, in Esau's cottage, from the dining table and various items in the disheveled bedroom. Victor had cataloged all these prints on lift cards and clearly identified each one: *Old Fitzgerald whiskey bottle, item #8 in notes.*

Victor had put yellow tape over the doors to the shower house and to Esau's cottage, along with the preprinted signs he kept in the trunk of his cruiser: *Crime Scene Do Not Enter by Order of Shawnee County Sheriff.*

He had taped off the area where the men had foolishly moved the corpse and carefully chalked around the body (his tongue most assuredly placed just between his front teeth as he always did when he was concentrating) so he could put down blue tape (the chalk would wash away with any rain that might come before the investigation was over, and the tape would not).

Victor had meticulously taken two rolls of pictures and cataloged each shot on his clipboard in his messy but legible handwriting:

Roll 1. Capability Fishing Camp.
Exposure 1. Ext. shower house facing entrance.
Exp 2. Int shower house taken from front entrance.
Exp 3. Int shower house, writing on back wall in red paint.

Dave stopped at the third one on the list and put down the clipboard full of notes and reports just as Victor approached.

"You go on back," Victor said. "I'll stay until Vashti is finished and we get him loaded up in the ambulance."

"I'm guessing we'll be meeting up later today to talk first impressions?"

"Yeah, let's take some time to think. Say six this evening? That'll give you a chance to get a little sleep. In the meantime, I'll get the family notified. Collins is good at stuff like that, at least."

"I'll see you then," Dave said. "But Nina took the boat on back, so I'm stranded."

"Take one of the camp's johnboats. I'll have somebody come fetch it later."

Dave started to nod but then thought that would be too polite. He didn't want to be polite to Victor, so he just turned around and headed toward the dock. Behind him, Victor called his name but he still didn't turn.

"What?" Dave said, as he walked away.

"Can we talk?" Victor called.

"No," Dave said. "Only about this case."

He could hear the resignation in Victor's voice when he said to his back, "I appreciate the help, Dave."

Dave found three metal johnboats nodding against one another in a slip down at the small dock. He knelt to untie one of them and saw Victor making his way back up the hill. He hated the pull his old friend still had on him. They had always told each other they'd remain best friends, no matter what. As teenagers they used to lie back on the hood of Victor's car and watch the stars and daydream about what they'd do when they grew up. Their hopes for their occupations and situations changed constantly, but the one constant had always been that they'd always be there for each other. And that's exactly what made it so much worse that Victor had betrayed him.

Chapter 10

Dave closed his eyes to relish the sun on his face. When he reopened them, he was taken aback by the deep blue of the lake on either side of him. Every day he was stunned at least a little bit by how beautiful it was. Not only the water, but also the rocky banks that made the lake so clean and clear, the green mountains rising along its edges, the lush smell of it all. Cedar Lake was known for possessing the widest stretches of any lake in the Tennessee Valley Authority. People often referred to its "big water," which he could look out and see right now.

He gripped the handle of the johnboat's sputtering Evinrude and even after a gruesome day he found himself feeling better than he had in a long while. He even found himself singing:

I said, you'll find my name on the tail of my shirt
I'm a Tennessee hustler and I don't have to work

He hated to admit that this newfound contentment, no matter how temporary it might be, was because he was working again. Hard to admit simply because he knew Victor was responsible for making that happen, and he didn't want to give him credit for anything.

The sky was the color of faded jeans and the rich smell in the air reminded him why this had been named Cedar Lake—tens of thousands, maybe hundreds of thousands, of cedars stood sentinel along its shores and constantly eased out their aromas. When he was a boy those cedars had stood at the tops of the ridges along the winding banks of the Big Laurel, the Cumberland, and the Wolf Rivers, whose green waters and round stones had been covered by the lake, just as the rich bottomland that had spread along their edges for centuries had been taken by the rising waters of the dammed rivers to make this lake. The old farmer had gotten him thinking about it but really, anytime he found himself loving the lake he couldn't help but to eventually come back to thinking of all that had been sacrificed to make way for it. Always his mind went back to the way the building of this lake had ruined the lives of so many of his parents' generation. They had not wanted to leave the valley to allow for the creation of the lake, no matter how many times they were told that their sacrifice would be in service to the country in making way for hydroelectricity, flood control, and tourism revenue. There had been bitter fights and legendary hold-outs.

Dave's favorite was the legend of Mamie Stewart, who had lived down in Lily Valley.

Mamie had refused to leave despite the government men going to her house many times to demand she did so. Her house was in the deepest part of Lily Valley, rife with laurel thickets so large men had gotten lost in them, and would be among the first of the places where the water would rise the quickest once Big Laurel River was dammed. Mamie had been eighty-three years old at the time. She had been born in the cabin that had stood here, three years before the Civil War started. During her childhood her parents had built onto the cabin, and later she and her husband had added more rooms and a clapboard exterior so one could walk in the front door and be in the 1930s, move through to the kitchen and be at the turn of the century, then go into the back bedroom and be transported to the 1850s. Mamie had given birth to her eight children in this house, and four of them were buried in the cedar grove a few yards outside her back door. She had suffered the hardest seeing their graves being dug up and carried away by the Corps of Engineers. People had thought she might give up after that, but her determination to stay had only grown fiercer.

The men from the Corps and the sheriff and his deputies finally had to go in full force to remove her. They carried her out of the house, kicking and screaming. One of her kicks caused the bottom of her shoe to stamp directly into the face of one of the men from the Corps, bloodying his nose, busting his mouth, and knocking him to the ground. After they helped him up, the other men got tickled. This infuriated Mamie even more, so she ran her long fingernails down the face of the sheriff, drawing blood.

"Laugh at that, you right bastard," she had said through her narrow teeth. Then Mamie fought off four grown men so she could run back into the house.

Just as the men were about to plunge in after her, she appeared in the doorway, clutching her guitar. "Take me to my daughter's house in Shady Grove," she said, and agile as a teenager she climbed up into the back of the Ford pickup in which two of the Corps men had arrived. There Mamie settled on a wooden peach crate with her back against the cab of the truck, the guitar perched on her knee.

The sheriff had pulled out first, turning on his blue lights as if escorting royalty up the mountain. "And really, he was," Dave's mother had always said at this point in the retelling. The truck followed the sheriff with the other two vehicles following closely behind. As the house faded from view and the gears ground in the truck as it climbed the mountain, Mamie began to play the first plaintive notes of "Gentle Annie" and sang:

> *You will come no more, gentle Annie,*
> *Like a flower your spirit did depart;*
> *You are gone, my lass, like the many*
> *That have bloomed in the summer of my heart.*

By the time Mamie reached the chorus, both the corpsmen in the cab of the truck had tears streaming down their faces and the driver told the other one he was sick of doing this work of removing people from their homes. "It ain't right," he said, and stopped at the top of the hill before the last glimpse of Mamie's home was out of sight so she could sing the rest of the song to her children's graves. When he did, she didn't move, but stayed on her wooden crate and kept singing:

> *Shall we never more behold you;*
> *Never hear your winning voice again*
> *When the Springtime comes, gentle Annie,*
> *When the wildflowers are scattered over the plain?*

The sheriff hadn't noticed them stopping and was barreling on up the road, but the two vehicles behind pulled close and listened through their open windows as she sang the last chorus. Unlike the men, Mamie did not shed a tear. Her face was as flat and hard as a gravestone. Later, the men told others that they'd never seen such defiance even as she finally accepted being removed. The driver ran his forearm across his face, unashamed of being so moved, and after a moment, they pulled away. In the back of the truck, Mamie kept her chin up and the muscle in her jaw tightened.

Dave could see down the lake to where a boat pulling two skiers behind it was crossing over the area where Mamie's house had been on a little patch of land that was now a hundred feet below water. That was the way of life, Dave reckoned: nothing was gained unless something was lost.

Just like Victor and Janet. Victor had lost his wife to cancer. Then he had gained a new wife in Janet. Which had caused Dave to lose his wife. As soon as he thought about this, Dave saw the issue: he was the only one who hadn't gained anything in the equation. Then he reminded himself of his freedom; he had certainly gained that, and on a pretty day like this, there were few things sweeter. On a day like this, he didn't even have to think about the lonesomeness that always loomed like a shadow over him. Or the fear of dying all alone with no one to mourn his passing. He certainly didn't want to think about that, so he gave the Evinrude a bit more gas and leaned back to continue singing his Jimmie Rodgers song. He belted it out, not giving a damn how well sound carried over the water, even over the high hum of the boat motor.

Chapter 11

Once Dave came to the buoys that stood guard around the Marie Marina to warn boaters to reduce to an idle, he eased the little johnboat over the smooth water toward the side of the marina where *The Sherlock* was docked. As he approached he could see Nina pouring coffee into a cup held out by Rex, who looked mighty happy with Shorty situated on his lap. Apparently Shorty noticed him about the same time because she went into her crazed barking that announced any visitor. Rex rubbed at her ears to calm her and waved.

By the time Dave had tied up the borrowed boat and made it to his own porch, Shorty was on the floor of Nina's porch right beside his, wiggling in anticipation of Dave scooping her up to offer some loving. He did just that. Shorty licked at his face and gave sweet little cries as if he had been gone for weeks instead of a few hours. He looked up to see Rex and Nina studying the two of them with humor.

"She missed Daddy," Nina said, and sat down at the porch table next to Rex. There was a spread that made his mouth water: glistening slices of tomato, crispy bacon, a bowl of poached eggs, and a rack of buttered toast. Nina snatched the coffee pot and poured a cup with a flourish then handed it over to him. "You surely need this."

"I surely do," Dave said, and savored the taste. "I'm glad you two are getting to know each other."

"Rex is pretty easy to get to know," Nina said. She had a smile that shined out of her face.

"I tend to make friends quickly with people who offer me a feast like this," Rex said, and shoved more bacon into his mouth.

"Go on." Nina nodded to the food. "Help yourself, Dave."

"You had enough energy to do all this without any sleep?" Dave said. "I'm beat."

"I got to catch a couple hours of shut-eye while you worked the case," she said. Lord, she was a pretty woman, and she looked fresh as a new morning despite her lack of sleep. Her red hair seemed even brighter in the sunshine and this made her green eyes seem brighter, too. "Then I woke up starving, and when Rex came by, he was good enough to join me."

Dave didn't have to be urged twice. He snatched up a plate and loaded it.

"You've had quite the morning," Rex said in his gentle way. Rex had once been a Catholic monk up at the Abbey at Gethsemane. He had left the coal mines of Northern England as a nineteen-year-old and had stayed at the rural monastery two decades, attending Mass six times a day, including at three in the morning. But then one summer day he was called to the office to be told that his mother had passed away. She had left him a large sum of money, which he was supposed to turn over to the church. As soon as he finished talking to his mother's attorney and hung up the phone, he realized he had spent twenty-five years praying and was tired of it.

"Just like that, I was done," Rex had told Dave one late night while they drank Jameson and looked out at the moonlight on the water. "Not because of the money, but because I realized I had missed my mother's whole life. I had given enough."

So Rex had left the monastery and walked south for three days until he came to the newly built Cedar Lake. He had been here ever since. He had used his inheritance to build the Marie Marina, a working memorial to his mother and now the most booming business in Shawnee County. He was likely one of the wealthiest men in the county, too, but no one would have known it by looking at him. Rex was a tall, handsome man with wavy brownish-silver hair that seemed to always be perfectly combed. He had a long, prominent nose that gave him an eagle-like look. "Aquiline," Dave had heard this sort of nose called. He didn't know where. Rex was one of those men who had no idea how good-looking he was and who seemed to become better looking the older he got. He must have been in his late sixties by now. He always wore a short-sleeved madras shirt, and, unlike any other man Dave knew, canvas shorts and sandals. The pale English skin that showed on his legs during the wintertime had no trouble becoming golden as soon as summer settled over the lake. There was something regal about Rex that went beyond his English accent. He carried himself with a sort of grace and he spoke to everyone calmly and evenly, still possessing the air of someone to whom you wanted to confess your sins.

"Bad business over yonder, from what Nina tells me," Rex said.

"The very worst business," Dave said.

"Murders around here are always about land or love," Rex offered. "Sometimes both."

"Not always, but yes, most of the time," Dave said.

"And sometimes people are just downright mean, don't you think?" Nina asked. "Out of their minds with the need for power or feeling slighted. Avenging something better left alone."

"I would agree with all of that," Dave said, and thought of Fogtown again. "And sometimes there's something more than just downright mean. Sometimes there's just pure evil."

"Nina said you were deputized. By Victor? Are you sure that's a fine idea, mate?" Rex leaned forward, fixing his storm-cloud–gray eyes on Dave's face in a way that made Dave hesitate to answer. If he was honest with himself, he'd have to admit that Rex was the closest thing he had to a father.

"It's good to be doing that work. I hadn't realized how much I missed it."

Rex raised his eyebrows, his way of saying he'd give it a week or so before Dave hauled off and knocked the hell out of Victor. Shorty was pawing at the hem of Rex's pants, so he scooped her up, gave her a kiss on her wet nose. "That's a sweet lass, she is." Shorty liked few people, but she loved Rex.

"Say, Rex, do you know anything about the phrase 'the sins of the father'?" The writing on the wall had been nagging at Dave ever since seeing it. He couldn't remember where he'd heard it before, but it sounded vaguely biblical to him. He had never been much on church and had only gone as an obligation when he was mayor.

"Well, it's all throughout the Bible."

"I thought so, but I wasn't sure."

"Some iteration of that phrase shows up several times. It's in Exodus, Deuteronomy, and Numbers. Ezekiel, too, I believe."

"All Old Testament books," Nina put in.

"That's right," Rex said. "You know your Bible."

"Not really," she said, "but after we moved to Alabama my mother got real involved in church and they gave us prizes if we memorized the books of the Bible. So I could recite them all in order at some point. Genesis, Exodus, Numbers, Leviticus, et cetera. That's about as far as I can go nowadays."

"But what's the context?" Dave asked, turning back to Rex.

"It's all about the sins of one generation passing down to another."

"You mean that the children of one generation are responsible for the sins of that generation?"

"Well, yes. For example, if your father kills someone and goes unpunished, the crime may be perpetuated on you, or you may be made to pay for it some way."

"Sounds like the idea of karma," Nina said.

"That's quite right," Rex said. "Except this is more generational than individually earned. And Deuteronomy refutes that notion entirely, basically saying that every man is responsible for his own sins."

"But the other scriptures uphold it?" Dave asked.

"There are contradictions throughout just about any holy text," Rex said, "but certainly in the Bible."

"But does that particular phrase itself show up in the Bible?"

"In the King James, which is the one most people use, the phrase is 'the iniquity of the fathers.' I don't really know how it's phrased in the lesser-used translations."

"But most people in these parts would use the King James," Dave guessed aloud.

Rex gave a little laugh. "I'd be surprised if anyone in these parts had even heard of any other version."

"This is all good to know," Dave said.

Nina let loose a little squeal, looking at her watch, and rushed up from the table. "I need to get into the office," she said. "You boys make yourselves at home and leave the dishes." Nina snatched up her purse and was about to leave when Dave called out to her.

"Please make sure you keep that off the record, about the message that was left," he said. "We don't need that out there right now."

"Of course, Dave," she said, and zoomed from the porch.

"I like her," Rex said. He cocked his eyebrow at Dave. "You do, too, I see."

"I've always liked her," Dave said. "We grew up together."

"That's not what I mean," Rex said. He poured himself more coffee and sat back as if content. "It's about time you got back into the world, Dave. She seems like a good opportunity for that."

"Slow down there, buddy. You just met the woman and you're already playing matchmaker."

"It's just that I know chemistry when I see it." Rex sat Shorty onto the porch floor and gave her ears a little rub. "All right, little Miss Shortcake, I have to get to work."

"And I should get a little bit of sleep," Dave said. He thrust his arms into the air for a stretch and felt his back pop in a good way.

Rex didn't bother to open the little door between the houseboat porch and the dock; he just swung his leg over. He put a hand into the air to say goodbye but then thought better of it. "Dave, at the risk of sounding like the wise old sage this morning, I want to give you one more bit of advice. All right?"

"I'm always glad to hear what you have to say, Rex."

"Don't let Victor—" Rex was struggling to find his words "—don't let him mess you about."

"This has nothing to do with Victor, and I'm not about to take any orders from him. I'm trying to solve a murder, not to help him."

"Then why?"

To help myself, Dave thought. *So I have something to do besides cleaning houseboat hulls in the daytime and drinking whiskey in the evenings.* But instead he said, "Because the crew he's got sure won't be able to do it."

Rex nodded. "You're a grown man, Dave. But I know how badly Victor hurt you. You can act tough all you want, but in some ways being betrayed by your best friend is even worse than being betrayed by your wife."

Dave had the urge to tell Rex that he wouldn't know since he'd given his whole life to the church instead of a woman, but he knew it was just his lack of sleep that conjured up this meanness in him. Rex was nothing but well-meaning. "Thanks for looking out for me," he said instead.

"Always will, mate," Rex said, and sauntered away.

Chapter 12

Dave hadn't been in a car in weeks, managing to fetch any groceries from the dock store and trying his best to not leave sight of the lake, but today he relished the slick feel of the steering wheel in his hands as he maneuvered the winding mountain roads between the marina and town. The Louvin Brothers were wailing on WCLC out of Burkesville where he usually kept his radio dial set. He loved their high lonesome sound, but he wasn't in the mood today so he switched to the Nashville station and there was good ole Hank Williams singing. That was more like it. Dave tapped his thumb on the steering wheel to the beat, surprised at how happy he felt. Soon he was driving down the hill into town.

Shady Grove was a town of 998 souls that straddled the Kentucky–Tennessee state line. The border ran directly down Main Street, which sometimes caused traffic to be stopped so tourists could have their pictures made standing on the yellow line. No one really seemed to mind, though. The lake brought business to town and most of the out-of-towners were so happy to be vacationing that they were mostly in good moods. Even the Yankees, generally.

This was a bright little town where the sidewalks were always swept, the two small parks on either side of town were always mown and full of overflowing flower pots, and houses actually had picket fences around their yards, gingerbread decorating their eaves, and American flags leaning from porch posts. On the surface the town was so perfect and wholesome it would have made a great postcard although the only postcards for sale on racks here were of the lake, of course. People in Shady Grove were proud of the lake, of their little town, and of their homes. Most everyone in town could trace their incomes to the lake or to the farms that spread out across the county around the town. These were good times for Shady Grove and its sister counties upon which it straddled. The building of the lake and the war, both completed a decade ago, had done well for the people, between the demand for crops brought on by the war and the hundreds of jobs brought on by the docks, the Corps of Engineers, the hydroelectric plant, and the dam.

Main Street was lined by neatly kept stores, many of which were outfitted with bright neon signs, such as Howard's Hardware; Baker and Butcher, where one could buy doughnuts, birthday cakes, pork chops, or baking hens; Newberry's department store; Ray's Ready-to-Wear, where mothers bought the clothes they couldn't make themselves for their children and husbands; Sue Ellen's Swell Closet, where the mothers treated themselves; the Hair Port Beauty Salon; and State Line Jewelry. Shady Grove possessed seven churches: Methodist, three different kinds of Baptist, one small Catholic church, a Church of God (which people just called "the holy roller church"), and on the very edge of town, an AME. The closest thing to a bar in town was the Shawnee Pool Room, which had a license to sell beer and did a brisk business in Stroh's and Pabst Blue Ribbon.

And there was the courthouse, looking more elegant than it had a right to, three wide columns supporting the high ceiling of its porch, surrounded by huge oak trees that had been planted in the 1830s and a towering Confederate memorial that had been installed sometime in the 1920s when the entire South started its nostalgia campaign for the Lost Cause bullshit. Dave never had been on board with any of that. And yep, there was the corner of the courthouse he had plowed into with his candy-apple-red Chevy on the night Victor and Janet got married and Dave had seven or eight too many glasses of Jameson. He was surprised to find he hadn't driven by here since the corner had been repaired. The brick was a slightly different color, but he wasn't sure he would've even noticed if he hadn't been the perpetrator himself. He had spent seven years working in that courthouse as the mayor but felt no allegiance to it whatsoever. He never had been right for that job and hadn't even known that he had done it all for Janet until the day he found out she was cheating on him.

As he paused at the stoplight he saw his replacement, the new mayor, Atlas Boone, waddling across the street in front of him in a three-piece suit and bowtie. He had the urge to honk the horn, just to give old Atlas a good startle for a laugh, but he kept himself from doing so. He didn't have anything against Atlas except that the man was so ineffective and boring, which actually was pretty perfect for his job. He had stepped into the role of mayor because he had been the vice mayor. As soon as a special election was held after Dave's resignation, Atlas had won handily since no one had been interested enough to step up and run against him.

Atlas was exactly what Shady Grove needed right now: quiet and calm. The most exciting aspect of the mayor's job was making sure there was enough salt for the icy sidewalks in wintertime and appearing at ribbon-cutting ceremonies for new businesses. Atlas and his little bowtie were perfect.

Dave turned onto First Street, then a right onto High Street where the three restaurants in town sat clumped together on one block: the Dixie Café, which served the best hot dog chili Dave had ever had (the smell of which was pumping out right now, causing his mouth to water), the Courthouse Diner, which served the best BLTs in either Tennessee or Kentucky, and Dot's, the only place in town that operated with cloth napkins and always had a good steak or fish plate on special. Then the sheriff's office, where he had served for three years before becoming the mayor. Those had been the good ole days. He'd had a great crew and a real passion for the work, especially the cases that kept him up at night. There hadn't been many murders during his tenure—only four—but he remembered each one in detail and he knew, without a doubt, that he had never been more alive than when working those cases. Especially the Fogtown case, which he still dreamed of sometimes. Who wouldn't, after the horrors witnessed in that house? At least he knew the killer was behind bars although he still shivered at the thought of such a monster still being alive in the world.

★ ★ ★

Victor was standing at the chalkboard in the conference room. Before him was the crew meant to solve this case: Dave, the only one with real experience on a murder case, Sheila Shepherd, who ran the sheriff's office and could have run the entire county if she set her mind to it, and Deputy Zeke Collins. Dave had always thought Zeke a dumbass but apparently he was good at rustling in suspects, which went a long way. He had just learned that Zeke had tracked down and captured Frank White, so Dave had to commend him for that—even though it seemed to Dave that Zeke was the one responsible for letting Frank run in the first place. Zeke was the kind of self-preening, arrogant cop who gave other cops a bad name. Victor had also called in Jimmy Storms, who worked traffic, simply because he wanted every resource he could get. Jimmy was an unassuming, hard-working fellow Dave had always gotten along with, the rare cop who seemed to enjoy the traffic beat. Jimmy was the kind of police officer who gave out parking tickets with a smile on his face, not apologetic but also never hateful about it.

Victor's hands were a dusty white from the chalk where he had been outlining the case. On the right side of the board was the victim's name: Esau Campbell. Below it, some of the details they had gathered:

36 years old
Never married
Cheating scandal
Black sheep of the family
Gambler
Drinker
Loner
Time Inside

On the left side of the board were the names of those present at the fish camp at the time of the murder:

Frank White
Tom Jenkins
Burgess Noble
Denise Rose
Ron Rose

Victor set the chalk in the narrow ledge of the chalkboard and wiped his hands together. Just as he was about to speak, the room shook with thunder and only then did Dave notice how much the summer day had darkened. A thunderstorm moved through just about every late afternoon in late summer, and this one looked to be a doozy. Lightning flashed. Victor paused just long enough to acknowledge the storm silently, then went on. "Dave, will you brief us on what we've got so far?"

Dave hesitated to nod or rise; part of him was miffed at the idea of Victor giving him power as another way to apologize. But there was a case to solve and no time for his feelings. Still, he felt awkward walking to the front of the room. Once there, though, he found his element.

"Our victim is Esau Campbell. Like the board says, he's the black sheep of his family. You all likely know about the Campbells—"

Every head nodded and Sheila scoffed in a way that signified what most people thought of the Campbells: they were so wealthy because they were also corrupt. Old Salem Campbell had been the state representative for this district for thirty years and hadn't done a thing for his constituents as far as Dave could see. For half his term Salem had been riding on the new economy that had come to the lake—a development that had nothing to do with him since the Tennessee Valley Authority had chosen where to put Cedar Lake because of the confluence of the Wolf, Big Laurel, and Cumberland Rivers, not because of any leadership on Salem Campbell's part. Everyone knew that Salem and his wife, Constance, spent most of their time in Nashville, but they had a huge mansion overlooking the lake and kept the trees cut back so everyone on the water would be able to see their wealth looming above them. To be a black sheep in that family was a badge of honor as far as Dave was concerned.

Now rain was pummeling the brick walls of the courthouse and pecking at the windows. These summer storms were always fierce and brief, but Dave hoped Vashti and her team had gotten everything they needed before the storm reached them.

"The Campbells have always had money," Dave said. "They were the biggest slaveowners in these parts before the Civil War and were in cahoots with every carpetbagger during Reconstruction. Made a fortune on mineral and timber rights they bought up from poor farmers. Salem's father, Edgar Campbell, was known for constantly disputing property lines so he could take land that didn't belong to him. But nothing made them richer than the creation of the lake. It was common knowledge that Salem bought up all kinds of land that he knew before anyone else would be lakefront property. Some of this he sold at top dollar once the Corps of Engineers offered federal money for it. That's why the Capability Fishing Camp has such a prime spot. When the lake was announced lots of people complained about him cheating them out of their money, but what he did was completely legal, even if it was unethical."

As Dave spoke the shower house wall rose up before him again, the red painted letters there: *Sins of the Father*. He had worked all this out on his houseboat porch shortly after his little nap, and had consulted with Rex to make sure his memory served him correctly. Rex was a walking encyclopedia of local history even though he had lived there only the past seventeen years. People just naturally told him things.

"Due to the message left at the scene, it's fair to think that Esau's murder was retribution for something his father might have done. Or, if we don't take the phrase completely literal then maybe even his grandfather or somebody else in his family. The phrase is from scripture and basically means that eventually, somebody in the family must pay for crimes committed by their ancestors."

Collins raised his hand, and Dave nodded to him. "So we ought to be looking at some of the people who were cheated out of their property." Collins might not be as stupid as Dave had first thought.

"Right," Dave said. "Let's start with who owned the land where the fishing camp is now. Sheila, can you pull those deeds for us?"

"No problem," she said, already scribbling a line on her list.

Dave figured he might as well stick with her while he had her. "Did you find any history on Esau?"

"Plenty," she said, and snatched a stiff sheet from the top of the stack of papers before her, prepared as always.

Sheila Shepherd was plain and messy and Dave kind of admired that about her: she refused to wear makeup and had never had any interest in pleasing a man in any way, shape, or form that he could think of. He couldn't recall ever seeing her smile although he didn't think of her as unfriendly, and she had a dry wit that had often made him laugh even if she didn't join in. "Dowdy" was a word people often used to describe Sheila, but he thought she was far too interesting for that to be accurate. He liked people who didn't participate in bullshit, and Sheila certainly did not. She wore dull brown or gray clothes, kept her hair pulled straight back tightly to be fastened in a neat ponytail, and almost always had a food stain on her blouse, but she was smart as hell and would work daylight to dark to help on a case. He also knew that she'd do anything for a friend; after he had resigned from the mayor's office, she had been one of the few people to reach out to him personally. She had showed up at the marina carrying an apricot nectarine cake she had made just for him, had plopped it down on his porch table, and without any sentimentality had said, "Don't let the bastards get you down, Dave" around the cigarette clenched between her teeth.

Now Sheila peered over her glasses and read: "Two drunk and disorderlies, ten years ago. In 1950 he got into a fight in Knoxville at a poker game and stabbed a man in the palm. Served a year for that, but he's been clean since. Looks like time in Brushy Mountain straightened him out."

There was a quiet ripple of laughter among the men. Brushy Mountain was notorious for "straightening out" prisoners. Known as the Alcatraz of the South, the prisoners there worked long shifts in the coal mines on its property.

Sheila looked up briefly over her glasses, unamused enough to hush all of them, and finished: "Ever since his release he's been managing the fishing camp and hasn't made a peep."

"Vashti has him in for autopsy right now, which might give us more, but she won't have toxicology for three days, even with a rush," Dave said. "Everybody I talked to said he had drunk plenty at the poker game but wasn't overly inebriated."

Already the storm had moved on. The gray clouds followed it and caused a swatch of sunlight to brighten the windows and wash over the rich maple wood of the tables where they sat.

Victor raised his hand and started talking as soon as Dave's eyes met his. "What are you thinking about the folks who were at the fishing camp?"

"None of them set off any alarms, but we don't have histories on any of them yet. I'm not ruling anything or anyone out yet. Noble and Tom have been to the fishing camp before, Tom many times. Denise Rose says that Esau said something suggestive about her to Frank when she was walking by him but says she didn't tell her husband about it. He claimed to have not known about it, but he easily could have heard the insult from his perch on the porch of their cottage. But still, even though that little altercation could provide motive, there's nothing to suggest either of them had anything to do with it. He discovered his mother's murdered body when he was a boy, though, he says. Sheila, can you check that out?"

Sheila scribbled and nodded.

"Would have happened in Dayton, Ohio in '25," Victor offered. "That leaves Frank. Any motive there?"

"Still digging. But only motive so far would be that Esau beat him badly in the poker game that night. And according to Noble he made a big deal about rubbing it in, too. And Ron Rose saw them arguing the night before that poker game, although they were chummy the next day when Denise Rose saw them together."

"And he ran off, which sure doesn't look good," Jimmy added, clearly set on Frank being the murderer even though he knew the least of any of them. "Looks awful guilty to me."

"A guilty man would have to be awful stupid to run like that, though," Dave said. "Shines the spotlight right on him."

"Good lord," Sheila said, her eyes still on the notes she was taking, almost as if she didn't intend to speak aloud. "What a puzzle."

Dave saw that Collins was slumped down in his chair, literally twiddling his thumbs. But he might as well give him a chance. "Collins, you've had more time with Frank than any of us. Learn anything?"

"Just that he's a cocky little sumbitch," he said, then wheeled around in his chair to lock eyes with Sheila. "Excuse my language, Sheila, but he is."

Sheila shrugged and rolled her eyes as if insulted that she wasn't being treated like one of the boys.

"You did a good job catching him, Collins," Victor said, and everyone nodded. Even Dave, almost unnoticeably. He and Victor had attended a session at a law enforcement conference years ago about the concept of positive reinforcement and how effective it was for team work, but Victor had taken to that more readily than Dave ever would. Dave had not been raised around people who gave you a pat on the head for anything short of lifesaving.

Collins spoke up. "Once I got him in the back of my cruiser, all he said was that Esau Campbell dying was a loss to nobody."

"He said it exactly that way?"

Collins nodded. "His exact words were 'a loss to nobody.'"

"What about during interrogation?" Dave asked Victor.

"Haven't done that yet," Victor answered and before Dave could grill him about it, he added, "I'll explain later."

Victor took them through all his crime scene analysis, which was mostly numbers, measurements, information that might come in handy later. Sheila took notes the most furiously. Collins nodded off a couple times. Dave wanted to slap the back of his head. Victor went on to say he had searched all the guest cottages and found nothing out of sorts. Nothing had been left behind in any of them.

"We need to start looking at the family," Dave said. "The father, Salem, first of all."

"Sheila, let's get him in here first thing in the morning," Victor said as he added Salem's name to the list on the board.

"I've called his office all day and the secretary says he's not come in."

"But you spoke to his wife?"

"I reached her at their place in Nashville, but she said she hasn't seen Salem in two days. From the sound of it, that's not unusual for the two of them."

Victor didn't like the sound of that; Dave could tell by the way he shifted his weight as he stood up there in front of the chalkboard. "Well, he's a state rep; he can't be that hard to get ahold of."

"And the stepmother—"

"Constance," Sheila offered, just as Victor started writing the name underneath Salem's.

"Yes. I'll go out and interview her tomorrow," Dave said. "Sheila, can you get Esau's siblings to come?"

"I think there's only the one, his sister. She just started college."

"Well, let's talk to her," Dave said. "Where is she?"

"The University of Kentucky, I believe," Sheila said.

"And she's not coming home to be with her family after this?" Victor asked.

"Maybe she wasn't close to Esau," Sheila said. "He was quite a bit older than her."

"I can't take the whole day to go up there for her. Jimmy, how would you feel about going up to interrogate her?" Dave knew he should've asked Victor before he put this forth to Jimmy, but he didn't care. Victor crossed his arms; miffed, but not enough to say anything.

Jimmy's whole body seemed eager. "Sure thing, boss," he said. "I'll leave at daylight."

Victor nodded. Sheila kept taking notes.

"And let's look into any romantic entanglements Esau's had over the past couple years. And I think that'll do it for now."

"All right, thank you," Victor said. "I appreciate every one of you." Just as everyone was in that first half second of rising from their seats, Victor added, "Dave, can you hang back just a minute?"

Dave sighed. He didn't have any desire at all to ever be alone with Victor, but on a case he'd have to on occasion.

Sheila noticed his discomfort. "How sweet to see the boys reunited," she said sarcastically, and gave him a droll look that was her way of laughing. She gathered her things and shuffled out.

The rest cleared out pretty quickly, anxious to enjoy the sweet air of a summer evening that had cooled down after the thunderstorm had sashayed over the lake on its way northeast.

Victor pushed his hands into his pockets and came closer, sat against the edge of a table a few feet away from Dave.

"Well?" Dave said. "Development?"

"I was hoping you'd interrogate Frank."

"Why didn't you do that earlier?"

"I thought it'd be good to let him dangle a little while."

Good idea, Dave thought, and stood. "Be glad to." He pushed in his chair, ready to go.

"But I want to talk to you a minute, Dave. Just about—"

"I told you, Victor, I'm not about to rekindle any kind of friendship. I just want to work this case, be professional when it comes to that, but on a personal level you can fuck right off."

Victor was unfazed by the insult. "I want to apologize this one time. Just give me that chance."

"I don't owe you a chance to do anything, Victor. Don't you get that?" Not knowing why, Dave pulled the chair back out as if to sit down, then shoved it harder back under the table. "I loved you like my brother and you took my wife away from me, behind my back—"

"It wasn't like that."

"Sure as hell looks that way," Dave said. "You're by God married to her now, and I'm not."

"Well, you're right. But. Grief messes you up, Dave. Glory was the love of my life. You know that. And when she died that way, I lost my mind for a little while. And I made the biggest mistake of my life, betraying you—"

"Yeah, you did," Dave said. "And I'm not going to forgive you, Victor. So save your damn breath."

Dave stomped out of the conference room. Sheila was waiting at the end of the hallway to escort him to the interrogation hall, papers clutched to her ample bosom as she drew hard on a cigarette. One small lift of her eyebrow let him know that she respected Victor about as much as he did when it came to personal matters.

Chapter 13

Dave entered the interrogation room without a word. He didn't even look at Frank White. He sat down before the prisoner and reached into the brown paper bag Collins had given him, then counted out the six hundred and thirty-two dollars, bill by bill. Five hundred of it was in one hundred dollar bills but the rest was mostly fives and ones, a couple twenties and one ten. Dave took his time, turning the heads of all the dead presidents in the same direction to give the collection added symmetry, but also to make a point to Frank, who let out a big sigh once Dave laid down the last of the cash.

"Well, Frank. It doesn't look good for you. You want to explain where this money came from?"

"The glove compartment of my vehicle," he said, and the emphasis he put on the *ve* in "vehicle" illuminated that he was from much deeper in the eastern mountains than here. If Dave was guessing, he'd say somewhere around Harlan County. Those were rough people up in there, hardened by the coal mines and the coal wars.

"Before that."

"Esau Campbell owed me five hundred dollars."

"So you knew Esau Campbell before this weekend?"

"I was down to the fishing camp back in March, when the trout were biting," he said, "and we got into a serious poker game. He bet too much and—"

"All right. So the five hundred is a debt owed from that. What about the hundred and thirty two?"

"The rest of it is my from my paycheck. I cashed it just before I came down here. The Clover Bottom Coal Company. You can check with them."

"I think you stole it from Esau Campbell's cabin this morning."

Frank scoffed, shook his head. "I don't need to steal. I work for a living."

"He beat you pretty bad at cards last night, I heard."

"Well, I beat the hell out of him the night before."

"Did he win back everything you'd won from him?"

"Just about. But that's the way it goes sometimes."

"You didn't have any hard feelings about it?"

Frank shook his head. "That's poker. If you can't take losing every now and then, you shouldn't play."

"And we have a witness who saw you two arguing a couple nights ago."

"We had words, but I wasn't the one who was angry."

"Then tell me about the argument."

"Like I said, he owed me five hundred dollars. Once I got there, he stalled on giving it to me and I told him I wasn't going to stand for it. He grabbed my wrist when I started to walk away and I shoved him back, told him he had an hour to get the money."

"An hour or what?"

"An hour or I'd knock his damn teeth out."

"People have been killed for less than that, owing someone that much money," Dave said.

"Well, I didn't kill anybody, and anyway he brought me the money within ten minutes, so we was square."

"And yet you played cards with him again the night after you'd had so much trouble getting what was owed to you."

"I've always had a hard time turning down a card game," Frank said, and leaned back, locking his hands behind his head, which accentuated the firm muscles in his arms. He was a man who had an easier time walking through life because he was so good-looking; Dave could tell that much.

"I understand that before the poker game, that morning, you and Campbell had a laugh at the expense of Mrs. Rose, the lady who was staying at the camp."

"The fishing champ?"

"There wasn't another woman on the premises that I know of."

"I was standing there having a smoke when she came out of the shower house. He said something nasty about her—"

"What, exactly?"

"He said, 'Look at the tits on that one.' Something like that. And I didn't say anything but I have to admit, she's a good-looking woman. So I might have looked at her, but I didn't have a laugh about her. I was just there."

"She says Esau called her a bitch because she gave the two of you a dirty look."

"She's telling the truth," Frank said. "But I don't see what that has to do with me. I don't like a woman being talked to like that."

"But you still played poker with him that night. He's already owed you money you had to twist his arm for, you don't seem to like him, yet you still played with him another night—"

"Look, mister, I came down to the lake to get some alone time. To do some fishing and sit around in the evenings and drink some whiskey. I needed to get my mind off some stuff. That's all there is to it."

At first Dave thought it was a bit strange for a young, handsome man like Frank to go away for a little getaway on his own, but in retrospect Dave should have done more of that back when he was married to Janet. Anytime he needed a break from her, he had always called up Victor to go somewhere: a drive down to Nashville to watch some baseball, shooting some basketball on the court behind the middle school, a chili bun at the Dixie Café.

"But something isn't adding up here, Frank. If you lost money to Esau on the last night he was alive, then how do you still have so much of it in your glove compartment?"

"The first two nights, I made big hauls in those games. The third night, I lost it all. But I had started out small; I didn't dip into my paycheck, I didn't dip back into the five hundred he had owed me. I'm not that stupid. I've got a family to support."

"You married?"

Frank nodded.

"So you needed some time away from your wife?"

"No, no." Everything about the man softened then: his voice, his face, even the tightness in his shoulders. "Never. She couldn't come with me and, I had to, I, well—"

Dave saw he was clamming up now.

"Come on, spit it out."

Frank was shaking his head, no, like a child who refuses to tell a secret.

"This is serious business. You ran away from an active investigation where you had been ordered to wait by the county sheriff. This isn't something to play—"

"Our daughter is sick. Bad sick. And she ain't gonna last long. I know it's wrong of me to leave them at a time like this, but I just can't face it. I'm just not as strong as my wife. And she told me to go away for a few days." There were tears in his eyes now. He wasn't allowing them to be shed, but they were glistening on his eyes. "It's hard to admit."

Dave didn't think the man was lying and besides, it'd be easy to check this out anyway. He didn't say anything but rose, went out into the hallway and snatched a mug off the little wooden stand, then poured it full of black coffee from the percolator Sheila kept plugged in all day long out there. When he went back in, Frank had collected himself, but Dave couldn't help but to notice the tremble in his hands. Dave sat the chipped cup of coffee in front of him, but Frank didn't touch it.

Suddenly Frank started to slap himself on his forehead with both hands. Smart, sharp sounds. Full-force hits.

"Whoa, whoa," Dave said.

"I'm so stupid! Stupid, stupid, stupid!" With each word he slapped his head again. Either this guy wasn't all there, or the grief over his daughter was taking him to a dark place.

"The problem is that you ran off, Frank," Dave said, his voice firm. He couldn't let Frank see that he had been moved by his situation. He had to plow forward. So what if his daughter was dying? Maybe that had fueled some deep anger in him that caused him to stab a man to death and write some words on the wall to throw the cops off his trail. "Now why the hell would you do that unless you had something to hide?"

"I was stupid. I was tired of waiting around for you to talk to me. I'd been there all morning and I wanted to go home. I needed to get back to my girl. I told my wife I'd be back first thing," he said, and put both hands into his curly hair as if he might pull it out by the handfuls. "I know how stupid it was, to leave. I tried to explain to that little deputy, and he just told me to shut up. He's a prick, that one. Held his gun on me for no reason. He slapped me, for no reason. Light little slaps that won't leave a mark but just startle you. Little bastard."

It didn't surprise Dave to hear that Collins might be one of those cops who acted docile around the boss but paraded his power when he could flash his badge to a civilian.

"You're gonna risk getting arrested and suspected of murder just because you're impatient?"

"I told you, I know it was stupid," Frank said, his tone so suddenly humbled that Dave almost believed him. "But I'm telling you, mister. My girl, she's real sick. And sometimes that doesn't make you think right about anything. I shouldn't have left them, and I've known that every day

I've been down here. I go out to fish every morning, and I don't even bait a hook. Just sit there and stare at the water and think about what's going to happen to us when she dies."

This guy was getting to Dave, but he had to stay on course. "If you'd just waited you'd be on your way home by now, Mr. White. But since you ran off, you've given us cause to hold you."

"What?" Frank's eyes grew wide. "You can't make me stay here." He raised his voice: "I didn't kill that man!"

"I don't have any other choice until we get everything you've told me checked out."

"I need to call home! That little asshole deputy dialed it and said nobody answered, but he's lying. They're *always* home. I need to call my wife and check on my girl."

Dave stood and went out the door, closing it gently behind him. He let out a long breath as he heard Frank fall apart crying behind the door. He bent around the doorframe of Sheila's office. She looked up but didn't crack a smile, of course. Just raised her eyebrows as if to say, "Well, what?" Dry as ever.

"Sheila, get that man a phone call home as soon as possible," he told her. He held out a piece of paper where he had written down what she needed to know. "And I need you to call his employer and check out these items for me."

"Got it," Sheila said, and looked back to her work, then suddenly back up. "Oh, I got some juice on Ron Rose. Everything on his story checks out. Mother murdered by his father when he was eleven years old, father killed in prison a year later by a cellmate. Mr. Rose was raised by his grandmother."

"Sounds like there's a 'but' coming."

"*But*," Sheila continued, "there was a lot of suspicion surrounding the case at the time. For a while, Rose was the main suspect."

"When he was eleven years old?"

"They had no real evidence on the father, but all kinds of things that didn't add up about the boy: the blood splatter on him, the way he reacted at the scene, some bruising on his wrists that suggested someone might have held him off. It wasn't a clear-cut case until the father confessed—"

"Which he may have done to protect his son," Dave interrupted.

"That's what I thought. And it's what some of the cops thought at the time. I talked to one of them who worked the case back then. Real old-timer, tough as a pine knot city cop, and he said it never did sit right with him."

"Good work," he said.

"That's not all. Ron Rose has no criminal record at all, but his wife does. Ten years ago, Denise Rose hit a man over the head with a paddle and cracked his skull. She was charged with assault and spent two days in jail, paid a fine. But the case never went further once he recovered and she claimed she had done it because he was trying to force himself on her."

"That sounds like her, based on the short time I had with her," Dave said. "She's someone who's going to always stand up for herself, and she's operated for most of her life in a man's world."

Sheila wasn't impressed. "Still, shows a violent streak. Apparently she knocked the hell out of him. The man had twelve stitches in his scalp and almost went blind."

"You're right," he said. "Really, Sheila, great work." It wasn't positive reinforcement if someone went above and beyond like Sheila always did. "Let's see if we can get the police down in Alabama to keep eyes on them while they're at that fishing tournament. I want to know where they are."

"We should be able to pull that off," she said, and turned back to leaf through her files, already ahead of him. "I'll check out the Frank White story and call you at the marina office."

"Good night," he called as he walked away, but if she replied, he didn't hear her.

Chapter 14

Rex was swaying in place, eyes clenched shut and singing along with the Ink Spots record that was spinning on his phonograph:

I don't want to set the world on fire

His voice was a rich baritone that went high on "fire". Dave thought he had such a good voice that he had missed his calling. Despite this, Rex didn't like to sing in front of people unless he was drinking. Tonight he was drunk enough to perform for Dave and Nina, who were captivated by him. There was a pining in Rex that he only put on full display when he was singing. More than a pining, really. A sadness. Rex never would tell Dave what had moved him to become a monk, but Dave knew that something bad had happened to him back in England before he joined the religious order.

Everybody was carrying some kind of grief. The older he got, the more Dave thought about all the trouble in the world. Sometimes there was just too much sadness. If a person thought too much about all the sorrow and despair and hunger and suffering in the world, they'd crack up.

Sheila had been able to confirm Frank White's story about his daughter with a quick phone call and had left a message with Rex before Dave even got back to the marina. The White girl was thirteen years old and dying of leukemia. He hadn't stopped thinking about her since learning this, even while he, Nina, and Rex were having a good time on Rex's boat. As badly as he hated to think that a dying girl's father was being kept away from her, the possibility was too rich that he had either killed Esau or had something to do with it. Frank would have to stay there for a while longer.

Dave wasn't drinking tonight although Rex made the most delicious gin and tonics he had ever had. One of his secrets was that he grew rosemary in a big planter on the top of his houseboat. He babied that rosemary plant year-round, watering it, talking to it, and the stalks made the gin come alive. Rex had spent some brief time in Spain as a teenager and they were always putting herbs in cocktails, he said. Dave was strictly a Jameson's man unless Rex was making the drinks, and Rex *only* drank Tanqueray. After he had run his car into the courthouse and humiliated himself, Dave had decided he would never drink more than twice in one week. He had grown up with an alcoholic; he wasn't about to be one himself.

The music faded away and Rex gave a little bow. Nina clapped wildly, snapping Dave out of his thoughts so he could join in on the applause.

"Rex, your voice is *so* beautiful," Nina said.

"That's kind of you to say," Rex said, blushing. Dave knew Rex did not like compliments much but was too polite to tell Nina this. Rex held up the green bottle of gin. "Freshen you up?"

"Please do," Nina said, and handed him the heavy highball glass in which he always served his drinks.

Dave looked out at the blackness of the lake, striped by the reflection of the waxing moon. The cedar and water scent of the lake came to him on a breeze and smoothed over his face. Such a beautiful night, but all he could think about was the case. He kept turning over the suspects in his mind and he kept feeling like something was missing.

"Are you still with us?" Nina was saying.

"What's that?" Dave mumbled. "I'm sorry. I was a thousand miles away."

"I can tell," Nina said, and Rex was looking at Dave in a way that signaled he agreed and was concerned.

"I know you have that no-drinking-two-nights-in-a-row rule, but maybe you should break that tonight. It's been a hell of a day."

"Just this once," Dave found himself saying, and after a couple drinks they were all laughing and singing even more. Rex put on Tennessee Ernie Ford singing "Sixteen Tons," and they all knew every word. The case was still right there, just slightly out of his grasp, but he was able to relax and enjoy the company of these two.

Dave was amazed by the way he and Nina were able to pick up their friendship so easily after all those years. They had been such good friends as children, but even as adults they were so alike that being with her felt like slipping his hand into an old glove he had misplaced for a few years but still fit perfectly. Her twinkling green eyes, pretty mouth, and curvy figure didn't hurt, either. But mostly she was just a lot of fun. Easygoing. A full-throated laugh. Good natured and so comfortable in her own skin that she made him feel comfortable, too. Rex certainly had liked her right from the get-go, and Rex didn't like too many people at all. Same for Shorty, who normally didn't like anyone except Dave and Rex.

Before he knew it, Dave had had three gin and tonics and the world was spinning. When Rex put a Bill Haley record on the player, Dave spun Nina around the small space of the houseboat porch, catching twirling glimpses of Rex laughing and clapping along, drunk as Cootie Brown himself. And the next thing he knew, he was stumbling back down the narrow dock, leaning on Nina, who didn't seem to be affected by the drinks at all. When they reached their boats sitting there side by side, she said, "Come in for a nightcap" with a certain kind of smile and he found himself following her onto her boat. She dropped a needle onto her record player and kicked off her shoes as she twirled to the trumpet of Chet Baker. By the time Chet had started singing, Dave found himself falling into her bed, where her freshly washed sheets smelled like lavender.

Then her lips were on his while Chet sang about "that old feeling." He sobered a little at that, became more attentive as she put her hands around his neck and climbed atop him, kissing him so hard that she briefly drew blood from his bottom lip. But neither of them minded. They were both overcome with hunger that had been brewing for a long time. He kissed her neck, then he kissed the tops of her breasts before she grabbed hold of him, pulling him back up to kiss her lips more. A stripe of moonlight laid a rectangle across her green eyes.

She slid her hand into his pants and took hold of him then, a hardness that hardened all the more once she tightened her grip on him.

She unbuttoned his shirt slowly, then thrust the sleeves down his arms so she could be rid of it, running her hands over his chest and bending to kiss him there, too. She pushed him back so she could take off his pants and spent a minute studying him down there, lightly kissing him from groin to belly button. Janet had never done anything like that, and it spent sparks flying up from the bottom of his feet.

After a moment she stood on her knees in the bed and put her arms up so he could pull her sleeveless dress over her head. He did this gently, then threw the dress across the small room in such a violent rush that she let out a laugh. She straddled him and they were moving together, skin on skin, feeling of each other in every way they could, with every part of their bodies.

He had to pace himself to make himself last. He wanted to please her, and eventually he did, causing her to let out low moans as she arched her back and sank her fingernails into his right shoulder so deeply that he was sure she had punctured the skin, although she had not. She was being so loud that he was sure other people on the dock could hear her. He hoped Rex couldn't. But then he didn't care. He was drunk and floating and this past year had been hell, so why not have some fun? He let go of a deep moan, too.

Afterward they lay beside each other breathing so hard that Nina got tickled. Dave joined in, laughing with her.

"I had a crush on you when I was a little girl," Nina said. "You must've known."

"I did."

"You forgot our kiss? You were my first."

He had never forgotten that. Most of all he had not forgotten how she had initiated it, down by the creek when all the other kids had scampered on home at suppertime but they had stayed behind, neither of them eager to go back to their parents.

"My first, too. And then didn't have another one for three years."

"When you were thirteen?" Nina laughed. "Late bloomer."

"I guess I was," Dave said.

"I thought about you when I was a teenager," she said. They were both watching the reflection the moonlight was making on her houseboat ceiling. "I never stopped thinking about you. Is that creepy?"

"No," he said. "I never forgot you, either."

"I just always wondered about you. And you ended up just as handsome as I imagined you'd be."

"You're not so bad yourself," he said.

The lake lapped against the side of the houseboat, making a pleasing sound.

Nina sat up in bed and felt around on the nightstand until the flare of a match briefly lit up the room. She blew out the match with the smoke from her cigarette. "But listen, Dave, I'm not interested in a relationship or anything. I've always wanted to be on my own. Do you think that's

Chapter 15

Lily Berry was watching her parents as they sat up there in the shade of the willow trees where they had a good view of Cedar Lake and Lily herself.

Lily was a very good swimmer, especially for an eleven-year-old. Her father had grown up on the river that had once run right through here before the lake covered it and most everything else he had known his whole life. He talked about it so much that sometimes her mother had to ask him to hush in that laughing little voice she had when she wasn't sure if she'd make him angry or not.

"Lily! Come back in, now!" her mother yelled, putting a hand over her eyes to block the bright morning sun. "You're out too far."

"I can still touch!" she said, stretching her leg so her toe just barely brushed the cool rocks below. As much as she loved to swim, she hated to feel the bottom of the lake. She was always afraid of what she might step on, like a broken Coke bottle or a lazy snapping turtle or a squishy rotten log that had sunk to the bottom.

"Come closer to the bank." Her mother was scared of water.

"Do as your mama says, Lily," her father said, calm and even, although that could always change as quickly as a match being struck, so she obeyed immediately. He had not really wanted her to swim today, anyway; he had said it was too early and that the water would be too cold. But when he was in a good mood Lily knew how to charm him into getting her way, and he had finally relented and let her jump in. When he had said he was going down to the lake to do a little fishing instead of going to church earlier that morning, she had begged him to take her with him, and when he agreed she had secretly put on her bathing suit, then a sundress to hide it. Her parents had laughed at her clever sneakiness when she revealed she had come prepared.

Her father was sitting up there on the bank beside her mother, looking uncomfortable. He was so busy watching her that he hadn't even baited his hook yet. She knew she would have to swim in closer to the bank or they'd make her get out.

"Is it not cold?" her mother called.

The water was warm as a bath to Lily. She lay on her stomach and brought one arm over, and then the other, turning her head with each stroke the way she had seen the girls in the news reel preparing for the 1956 Summer Olympics, which would be held next year in Australia.

Lily loved the silky feel of the water as she swam through it. To swim felt like floating, or flying, or being in a dream.

She loved the lake, too. She loved how clean the air smelled here, and the way the birds sang louder on the little islands, and the thin, slender rocks on the banks, rocks her father had taught her to skip across the waves so they skidded along six or seven times before sinking.

She had grown tired and was treading water, careful to keep her legs up so her feet wouldn't drift down and touch the bottom.

They only lived a few miles away, but these days they came to the lake less often. Not only did her parents work all the time, but now her mother was going to have another baby although Lily didn't want her to. She hadn't told anyone this, though.

"Lily," her father said, standing up now. "I'm not going to tell you again. You're out too deep."

Lily did a backstroke toward the bank. The sun was hanging low in the western sky and had painted the still water a soft gold. Right out there is where her father had grown up during the Depression, in a little valley that was way way down beneath the lake now. Once he had stopped the boat out there and pointed down and said, "That's where your daddy was raised." Lily couldn't even imagine how this was possible, no matter how many times he had explained about the way the river had been dammed to make the lake and how all the people living there had to leave.

The golden light on the water looked like a dream that might swallow her up. She wanted to swim out in the middle of *that*. They'd be mad if she went out that far, but it'd be worth it.

So she took off, swimming as hard as she could, the water churning all about her. But only seconds passed before she heard her mother screaming for her to come back and then she was aware of her father yelling, too. She turned to look just as she saw him run into the water toward her, wetting the legs of his jeans. So even though she was filled with determination to show them just how far she really could swim, she decided it wasn't worth setting off one of his temper explosions. She gave up and stopped, pedaling her legs and taking deep gulps of air.

Lily's father saw that she had stopped, looking angry until she saw him decide to try not to be. "You're crazy, girl," he called to her, not quite smiling, but not angry either. "What do you think you're doing?"

"I wanted to swim all the way out to where you used to live."

"That's too far." Concern gathered on his face and in his voice again. "Now come on back."

He stood there with his feet in the water—she could see his discarded shoes on the rocky shore behind him, where her mother was nervously pacing, one hand cupping her pregnant belly like always. She had put on her prettiest maternity dress—pink, with a frilly collar like the doilies on Lily's grandmother's coffee table—even though they were coming down to the lake bank. Her mother had said on the way down it didn't feel right to be casual on a Sunday morning.

"Come into the shallows, now," her father called, "so I can do a little fishing."

Lily minded him, but before she reached the place where she could touch bottom again, she paused for some reason. She never would figure out why. Years later she would wonder about that.

Then Lily was aware of something moving toward her. It was more of a feeling than anything else until she saw it. Something very white and large coming up out of the water.

She couldn't believe what she was seeing even as she realized what it was. And she couldn't make herself move away.

A body was rising from the bottom of the lake.

A man, face down, his two grayish-blue arms reaching toward her as he rose, rose, the white collar of his shirt pulsing like a fish's gills when they are out of water.

A scream was caught in Lily's throat, but she couldn't move her legs or her arms or her mouth. Even as she was frozen, the deep water was pulling her back out toward it, away from the bank. She felt like a dry towel had been pushed down her throat.

As the top of his head neared the surface of the water, his hair expanded and moved like jellyfish she had seen in the World Book. She and her friends did this sometimes: stayed still in the water with their hands before them, face down. Dead man's float, they called it.

Except this man really was dead. She could tell.

The body began to turn onto its side and she was still frozen so she could not move before his face was revealed to her, but all that registered for her were his eyes. They were open and rolled back in his head so that only the whites showed.

Then something in her mind broke and she could hear her mother screaming and her father yelling and splashing toward her. Lily couldn't breathe or swallow or move.

The dead man was looking right at her—right *through* her—and his arms were reaching out for her and when one of his icy, slick hands slid down the length of her leg his arm got latched around her somehow, and even as she was thrashing away from him, she was being pulled down. She could feel the long, heavy length of the dead man lying right on top of her as she went down beneath him. She was screaming out—she could see a blast of bubbles rise in front of her—but then water rushed in and she choked on it, pulling in a rush of the lake.

But at last her father plucked her away from the dead man. He swam with one arm and held her in the crook of his other, then he was carrying her in his arms the way he used to carry her to tuck her in when she was very little. He laid her on the bank and worked on her, holding her nose and blowing air into her lungs. Her mother fell onto the ground beside her and she kept saying Lily's name over and over. Then the water came out like hot vomit and Lily started screaming.

She started screaming and she couldn't stop.

Chapter 16

Dave came to with his head throbbing, the sun bright in his face, Shorty's sharp, high barks tearing through his skull, and the slow realization that someone was pounding on his door. Dave arose bleary-eyed, clad in nothing but his Fruit of the Looms, and tore open the door to find Rex standing there with a judgmental look on his face.

"You're the one who talked me into drinking," Dave said.

"Get some clothes on," Rex said, turning away. He hated when people slept late. "Victor called and he needs you to call him back. There's been another murder."

Relief washed over Dave as he tugged on a pair of Levi's and buttoned a shirt onto himself. Relief because another murder meant that their suspect list was now greatly narrowed. Frank couldn't have done it since he'd been in jail. He'd be able to send the man home to his troubled family. The Roses couldn't have done it since they were in Alabama for the fishing tournament; the police down there had been keeping a close eye on them, and Sheila had checked in with them twice.

He tucked Shorty under his arm and carried her to the end of the dock. He sat her down on the bank so she could do her business and kept his eye on her through the window while she sniffed around in her best detective impression.

All of his relief was dashed as soon as he spoke to Victor.

"Vashti thinks the body's been in the water about three days."

"Three days. So this would have happened before Esau was killed."

"Right. And the kicker is that it's Salem Campbell."

Dave blew out a breath—now this was something. "Esau's father."

"Yep," Victor said.

"Well, that certainly makes it more interesting," Dave said.

Dave could hear Sheila talking to Victor in the background before Victor apparently capped his hand over the phone. There was a brief silence before he came back on. "Listen, Dave, we've got a lot going on here, but would you go over to the Campbell place and interview his wife, feel it all out, and track down whoever else in the family you think needs talking to?"

"Has she been told yet?"

"Not about Salem. Sheila managed to track her down yesterday to inform her about Esau. She was staying at their place in Nashville, and Sheila said she was upset when she broke the news."

"Even the black sheep of the family stays a part of the family, I reckon," Dave said. He was desperate for a cup of coffee and saw that a tea pot was standing on Rex's desk.

He lifted the lid and found that it was empty. "So she's back from Nashville now?"

"Yep, they got to the Campbell mansion on the lake last night," Victor said. "If you don't want to tell her about Salem, I can have Zeke—"

"No, I'll do it," Dave said. Interviewing was what he liked best, and he knew it's what he was best at doing. That had been the key to solving the Fogtown murders all those years ago.

"Can you get down there soon? Word about this will get around right quick, and I'd rather she heard it from us first, in person."

"I can be over there within twenty minutes," Dave said, glancing at the clock on the wall above Rex's desk. "Who found the body?"

"Steve Berry."

Steve ran the Dixie Café, just as his father and his grandfather had. The Dixie Café had been a fixture in Shady Grove for the past thirty years or so.

"Actually, his little girl. Steve had taken her swimming down at the Flatwoods and she got tangled up in the body."

"Jesus."

"Yep. She's only eleven. Scared her to death."

"I bet," Dave said. "All right, I'll call you once I know something."

As soon as Dave hung up, he realized it was the most cordial conversation he'd had with Victor since his whole world had fallen apart because of him.

Shorty was hunched and barking on the bank, the dark hackles on her back at attention. Dave skipped across the wooden walkway to pluck up the dachshund, who was about to have her nose snapped by the turtle she had cornered in the crevice between two rocks.

When he came back onto the dock, Rex was outside the marina office, wiping down the gas pumps. "Heading out?" he asked.

"Yeah," Dave said. "I need to run over and interview his widow. All right with you if I wait to clean those johnboats up this afternoon?"

Rex nodded.

Dave went back to the boat, desperate for a cup of coffee before he headed out. As soon as he reached into the cabinet to feel for the glass jar of Taster's Choice, he remembered that he had used the last of it and had intended to buy more on his way to the meeting but had forgotten. "Son of a bitch!" he hollered, and slammed shut the cabinet. By the time he was ready, Shorty had already gone back to bed for the day, as she often did in the late morning. She was snoring away under her little blanket in her bed that sat on the floor next to his.

He threw a couple of aspirin into his mouth, chased them with a whole glass of water, then gulped down a handful of potato chips, thinking they might help to steady his stomach. He grabbed his notebook and a pencil and rushed out, only remembering his car keys once his feet left the boat and touched down on the dock's walkway. He ran back in and snatched them up. As he flew past, he noticed that Nina's houseboat was empty; she had most likely gone into work early this morning. He wondered if her hangover was as strong as his. Probably not since she had not drunk as much as him and certainly had not been buzzing as hard as he had been. His head was killing him and the bright sun reflecting off the green waters of the lake wasn't helping matters at all.

On his way out he stepped into the marina office, where Rex was leaning back in his chair, the newspaper spread wide before him. The front page headline was written out in a dramatically large font: BRUTAL MURDER ON THE LAKE.

"I shouldn't be long but if I'm not back within a couple hours, can you check in on Shorty?"

Rex's face was hidden behind the paper. "Yes, and I'll take her up the hill for a loo break."

"I appreciate it."

Rex gave the newspaper a shake that allowed him to more easily fold it in half. "Our Nina is quite a reporter," he said. "A very thorough article about the murder in today's *Sentinel*."

"I'll have to look at it later," Dave said. "I've got to go."

Rex nodded to the bowl of fruit on his desk. "Take a banana," he said, and looked back to his paper. "It might help with that hangover."

Chapter 17

Everyone knew where the Campbell Place was, even though the mansion couldn't be seen from the road. Everyone on the lake had seen it, though, as it sat on a high bluff looking over the wide waters.

As Dave drove down the winding driveway to the estate, he thought of the scene in that Hitchcock film *Rebecca*, where the unnamed heroine is taken to Manderley for the first time. The Campbell Place might not have had a fancy name, but it was along the same lines of wealth and grandeur. One last bend in the road, and there was the home of white brick and roof of six gables. The windows were long rectangles of double-paned glass and metal frames. The porch was supported by several columns, populated with wrought iron furniture and several concrete planters full of healthy red geraniums. He parked and crunched across the pea gravel toward the front door, which was abnormally wide and tall, made of solid maple and outfitted with a large knocker in the shape of a fox. He didn't have time to use it before the door was snatched opened by an old lady in a plain blue dress that somehow suggested a uniform in its starchiness. A maid, he thought. He didn't believe he had ever seen a servant in real life before, only in movies.

"How may I help you, sir?" Among the deep wrinkles, the violet eyes of the old woman glowed out at him.

"I'm here to see Mrs. Campbell, ma'am," he said. "I'm afraid I have some bad news."

"She's already been told about Esau, sir." She started to close the door as if the conversation was over, so he stepped forward, planting his foot on the threshold. She glanced down in surprise, then looked back up to lock eyes with him. This lady had a calm demeanor, but he could see she was no pushover. "She returned just this morning to start the arrangements. Mrs. Campbell is upset and doesn't want visitors."

"Unfortunately, this isn't about Esau," he said. "I'm Deputy Hendricks, sent by the sheriff."

The woman looked hesitant, but relented. "Come in, sir."

"And who are you, ma'am?"

"I'm no one," she said and hesitated, to see the expression on his face. Although he thought this a strange—and sad—thing for anyone to say, he didn't allow his look to tell her anything, even after she went on. "I'm the housekeeper, Carol Ann Gabbard."

"Glad to know you," he said.

She pointed to the floor just inside the door. "Wait here, please."

She scurried away, her bent back suggesting a long-standing spinal problem, and Dave took in his ornate surroundings. The foyer was tiled, and in the middle of the floor was an antique table holding up a huge china vase crammed full of various flowers that one might see in a florist's window but which he suspected came out of a well-maintained garden somewhere out back. A glistening chandelier hung above him. The rooms on either side of the foyer looked like living rooms, but he imagined they each had their own purpose. Both contained sturdy furniture, Oriental rugs, and fresh flowers. A black-lacquered baby grand piano stood in the room to his right. Everything appeared to be freshly polished.

Again he was reminded of mansions he had seen in the movies because he had certainly never graced them in real life. Dave had been raised poor and even as mayor had never had much because he'd had to start from scratch. People raised with money didn't understand the way most of the world had to scratch and fight for everything they had, even once they had a good-paying job. The Campbells had always been rich, and always on the backs of others, whether it was slaves before the Civil War or the virgin forests around here the Campbell family had bought up and cut down during the building boom of the early 1900s or the loads of money they had made from all of the property they owned near the lake. He never had been comfortable around people with money, but at least he'd never had to be in their own territory; he didn't like being in this house one bit.

Dave didn't understand why anyone would want to live this way; the place had the feel of a museum more than a home. Every single thing was for show, and nothing appeared to exist for comfort.

The housekeeper appeared at the end of the hallway where she had disappeared earlier. She lifted an arm to beckon him toward her so she wouldn't have to yell, and when he was halfway down the hall, she said, "Mrs. Campbell will see you on the back patio, sir."

After the cool shadows of the house, the sunlight blinded him for a moment when he stepped out of the French doors and onto the large flagstones of the patio. Cedar Lake spread before him as he had never seen it before; this was certainly the best view of it anyone had. The politician's wife was sitting at a round wicker table with a beautiful breakfast lain before her even though it was nigh on lunchtime. Brunch, he had heard such a late breakfast called. There was bacon, toast, a sliced tomato, grits, a bowl of fruit. Her cutlery was still lying wrapped in a cloth napkin next to the plate of untouched food. Her eyes were raw from crying and she was still wearing her nightgown—the pink silk collar showed within the collar of her paisley robe—but even dressed this way, she was an elegant and beautiful woman. Early sixties, Dave guessed, and a full fifteen years younger than Salem. Dave knew that Salem's first wife had died twenty years before, but he knew very little about Celeste Campbell beyond the fact that people around here felt like they barely knew her. She did not show her face in town much and rumor had it she spent most of her time in Nashville, where they kept a big house in Belle Meade, the swankiest neighborhood in the city.

"Good morning," Dave said, but he had barely finished his sentence before she cut him off.

She unrolled the napkin containing the silverware and held the fork and knife in her right hand before placing them gingerly on either side of the plate. "Have you found who killed him?"

For a moment he thought she might already know about her husband's death, but he went with what Victor had told him and assumed she meant Esau.

"No, Mrs. Campbell. I'm very sorry to say that—"

"That was very rude of me, to just launch into it like that. I've just been so upset." She nodded to the other chair at her table and picked up the fork to drive its tines into a piece of cantaloupe. "Please, have a seat."

Just as he pulled out the chair, Carol Ann appeared with a coffee cup for him, situated on a delicate saucer. She sat it down, plucked up the silver pot, and poured for him with a flourish, pulling the pot high and then lowering it to the cup. The rich aroma rushed up to his nostrils and as much as he craved a drink of it, he knew this was not the appropriate moment for that.

"Ma'am, I'm Dave Hendricks."

"Please call me Celeste, Deputy."

"I'm a deputy for the Shawnee County Sheriff's Department, and I'm very sorry to tell you that your husband has passed away."

She didn't flinch nor say a word for a moment, but slowly her face took on the look of confusion. "Salem? But, Esau. Both of them?"

"Yes, ma'am. I'm very sorry to say."

Celeste rose quickly as if she was about to storm away, still holding her fork, but just as suddenly she sat back down. "But how?" she asked, calmly. "Not murdered, too?"

Dave nodded. "We believe he was killed a couple of days before Esau, ma'am." He wasn't about to call her by her first name. "But he was only found this morning."

For a moment she looked as if her face might crumble, but she gathered her strength. "My God," she said. "Where?"

"In the lake. At the Flatwoods."

While she thought about that, he thought it reasonable enough for him to take a drink of the coffee. By this time it would have seemed rude not to, and lord, the taste of it was like a balm. He could feel its warmth soothing his headache and his belly simultaneously. Still her face betrayed no real emotion, but that didn't mean anything to him. After being in a war, law enforcement, and politics he knew that everyone handled shock and grief in different ways. There were some tell-tale signs—someone who acted too distraught or a murderer who feigned surprise, for instance—but even those were hard to pinpoint positively. But since she wasn't breaking down, he might as well take advantage of getting as much information out of her as he could.

"I understand that he was supposed to be out of town?" he asked.

"Yes, on Friday afternoon he was supposed to leave to go to the state capitol for some meetings. I just assumed he was there. I went to Nashville early Friday morning. I had planned to stay there a week to attend some functions for the symphony," she said, as if it made her feel better to explain all this. "I'm on the board, you see, and we're having a big fundraiser tomorrow night. Then a concert the night after at the War Memorial."

"So this was pretty normal for the two of you? That he'd go to Frankfort or somewhere, and you'd stay here, or in Nashville?"

"Very normal. Salem was always off to some political gathering or business meeting. And I stay in Nashville, mostly. This is a beautiful house, Deputy, but it's also a very lonely place. Shawnee County is a beautiful place, too, but it's not exactly known for its social life."

Especially when your family has screwed over most people in the region, Dave thought. Yet these same people kept electing Salem Campbell to office, didn't they? Although nobody liked him much, voters here voted solely on party lines and the Campbells had held down that fort for decades now.

He tried to soften his tone as much as he could with his next question: "And normal for the two of you to go three days without speaking on the phone?"

She nodded.

"Even when you found out his son had been killed, you didn't try to reach him?"

"Of course I did," she said. "But I couldn't get him on the phone anywhere. The state house is closed on the weekend, so there were no secretaries to answer my calls. I called the house in Frankfort several times, but he never answered. We don't have servants there; all he ever does is sleep there." Celeste Campbell let out a long sigh that seemed to come from the bottom of her lungs. A sigh of complete exhaustion or anger—he couldn't tell which. "Do you have a cigarette, Deputy?"

"I'm sorry, ma'am, I don't smoke."

"Carol Ann!" The woman's elegance fell away instantly when she barked out the name of the housekeeper, who came scurrying in, head down, and scampered away as soon as Celeste cried out, "My cigarettes!"

Just when he thought the woman was not going to answer him, she looked him right in the eye. "Deputy, it was normal for the two of us to go much longer than that without speaking. Sometimes a week or two. There's no use lying about it: my and Salem's marriage was over a long time ago. Ten years ago or so." She snatched the red packet of Winstons away from the trembling hands of Carol Ann as soon as the servant reappeared and drew in from the flame of the silver lighter the little woman held before her. Suddenly she took the hand of the maid and tears were in her eyes. "Oh, Carol Ann. Salem's been killed."

"Oh, no, Celeste," the little woman said, and her pity sounded authentic to Dave, although he was intrigued to hear her call her employer by her first name. Celeste put one hand up against her shoulder so Carol Ann could take hold of it. She did, and put her free hand on the back of Celeste's head. "Oh, honey, I'm so sorry."

Dave took this opportunity to help himself to more coffee. The housekeeper stood behind Celeste in a strange, still tableau. Celeste wiped the unshed tears from her eyes and nodded firmly; this was enough to release the other woman from her stance. She scurried away.

Two jets of white smoke propelled from Celeste's nose. "We didn't like each other very much. I think that in your interviews you might be hard-pressed to find anyone who liked Salem. But still, he was—" She stopped, as if she couldn't find the words she needed, and propped her right elbow atop her left hand so the cigarette was level with her face. She held it between forefinger and index, her thumb lightly stroking the filter. "I'm not happy that he's dead. I didn't hate him. Most of the time. We loved each other, once upon a time. That's something, isn't it?"

He didn't know quite how to answer her question, so he pushed on. "So the last time you saw him was Friday morning when you left here?"

"That's right."

"And did you notice anything at all that was not normal?"

"Nothing. The same as always. We were here together a few days and he did his thing, I did mine. He was always working. Always on the phone. We saw each other at meals, barely spoke, but—" she paused here, choosing her words carefully. "I'm making it sound worse than it was. We had settled into our unhappiness and were fine with it. I read, listen to music, work puzzles. Sometimes our daughter visits from Lexington. I spend as much time in Nashville as I can and have plenty of friends there. I so enjoy my work with the symphony."

"And as I understand it, Esau was distanced from the family."

"From his father, yes. And Salem ruled everybody else, so if he said for us to not speak to Esau, we had to obey or sneak around. But I always liked Esau. His mother died when he was just ten years old, and Salem was never really there for him. He was nearly fifteen when I married Salem, but in the three years he lived with us, we were good friends. He made me laugh."

Then she collapsed into tears. She cried openly and messily for a minute, then dabbed at one corner of her eye daintily with the cloth napkin. Her grief appeared out of nowhere but not too over-the-top to be unbelievable. But still, he had seen some award-worthy performances in his time. He didn't trust anyone.

Dave sat silently until she had collected herself, then asked, "When did you last speak to Esau?"

"I saw him two days before he died."

"Why?"

"I stopped by to check on him on my way to Nashville. I did that every once in a while."

"And what time would that have been, ma'am?"

"Oh, early. I like to get on the road first thing. So around seven, I'd guess."

So, Dave thought, *she is who Tom heard arriving early in the morning.* "Anything unusual strike you there?" he asked.

"No. At first I was shocked by how spartanly he was living in that little fishing cottage. But it was all neat and orderly and—" she paused, sighed deeply while she considered if she should go on, then she did. "This sounds stupid, but I envied him, in a way."

Having been in Esau's sparse living quarters, he couldn't imagine this spoiled woman wanting anything her stepson had. "How do you mean?"

"The simplicity of how he was living. He had the cottage, a fishing rod, a few clothes, and that was *all*. He seemed more content than I've seen him since he was a child. The fishing camp suited him. Gave him some purpose, but not so much responsibility that it overwhelmed him." She gave a ragged laugh and kept her eyes on Dave's while she spoke. "Some days I'd like to run off and live in a little four-room house, to just get rid of all this *stuff*," she said, and drew her hand through the air to indicate the gardens, the mansion, the property. "I know, it's pathetic of me, isn't it? What was the title of that Shirley Temple movie?"

Dave didn't know; he was more of an Alfred Hitchcock or Westerns kind of filmgoer; the last movie he had loved had been *Shane*. He shook his head, although he didn't know how perceptible this motion appeared. She wasn't looking at him anyway. She was peering into the distance with her brow furrowed, trying to remember the name of the movie.

"*Poor Little Rich Girl.* That's what it was. That's what I sound like, a spoiled woman who doesn't understand how good she has it. But people think money solves all your problems. It doesn't."

Dave wanted to say that only people with money ever said that, but he remained silent.

"I wasn't raised with money, and it took me a long time to get used to having it. But once you get used to it—" She didn't finish. She paused, then took on another thought: "Esau always made bad decisions. Getting in a knife fight in Knoxville was the straw that broke the camel's back for

Salem. You can imagine how that played in the newspapers. The son of a state rep in prison," Celeste said. She most likely couldn't talk about any of this with her high society friends. "It almost cost him the reelection. Long before that, Esau had ruined Salem's hopes of having a political dynasty. He groomed Esau to follow in his footsteps, you see, and he went the opposite way."

"What about your daughter?"

Celeste laughed like someone at a cocktail party but the joy in the sound curved into derision. "Our daughter is a woman, Deputy."

"Not unheard of for a woman to enter politics. Rare, I know, but we've had women in Congress for forty years now, ma'am," Dave said before he could catch himself. It was not his place to offer such commentary, but he had been shocked by her attitude.

Her laugh was a short, twinkling thing. "You misunderstand me, Deputy. Those are Salem's words, not mine," she said. "He doesn't think a woman has a place in government. The irony is that our daughter loves politics. She's studying it, at the University of Kentucky. But that wasn't in the cards for Esau."

"Were Esau and your daughter close?"

"No, they never even lived in the same house. He was on his own by the time she was born, and Salem has always kept them apart. Esau wasn't the smartest and he pushed a lot of people away, but he was always sweet to me. We had soft spots for each other. I was always defending him, and he often took my side when I had arguments with his father." Celeste let out another shuddering breath.

"Does anyone come to mind that might have wanted to kill Salem or Esau?"

"I imagine they both had plenty of enemies," Celeste said. "Salem was a good businessman. I'll give him that. The best ones are the most brutal ones. And a shrewd politician. He has made a lot of people mad. And Esau—well, the way he drank and played cards doesn't exactly attract the best company, does it? He had a terrible temper, too. Esau's anger at his father seemed to just overtake his whole life."

"What was that anger about?"

"Have you ever noticed how people who are a lot alike have trouble getting along? They were both more alike than either of them wanted to admit."

"How so?"

"Stubborn. Short-tempered. But both with a desperate need to please those they love, whether they'll admit it or not. I think it was Salem's greatest heartbreak that he couldn't have a real relationship with his son. And Esau grieved for it, too."

"It seems clear that their murders were connected. Do you know of them having any kind of joint efforts or business dealings or anything of that nature?"

"Oh Lord, no," she said, and stubbed out the cigarette in the large ashtray. She shook her head. "That would have never happened. Salem would have never even let him run the fish camp if I hadn't orchestrated that. He gave him that job just so I would stop nagging at him."

"I hate to ask this, Mrs. Campbell, but do you know the particulars of your husband's will?"

"Do you mean am I the one who stands to benefit the most from the death of him and his firstborn?"

"I don't mean it that way, but—"

"Everything in that will goes to our daughter, Patricia. All the money, this house, this land. He left Esau the fishing camp, and that's it. As for me, only the Belle Meade house in Nashville and enough money to get by. He knew that's all I wanted, anyway."

Dave would have to wait until the courts released the will, but there seemed little use in her lying about this now since she knew the will would be read out soon.

"If you don't mind, ma'am, I have a couple more questions." Normally he wouldn't keep going with someone who had just been told their spouse was dead, but she was being plenty talkative. "I'm sorry to take so much of your time."

"When you leave, Deputy Hendricks, I'll be sitting here staring at the lake and thinking about my dead stepson and husband until my daughter gets here. So I am in no hurry to be alone."

"There's a photo in Esau's cottage that shows the fishing camp has lost some of its buildings."

"Yes, there was a fire. The store, and a couple of the cottages," she said. "The store went up first and the others were nearby enough to catch, too. This would have been a couple years before Esau took over."

"Was there anything suspicious about that?"

Celeste narrowed her eyes at this. "How do you mean?"

"Arson, maybe? Or something else?"

"The fire inspector declared it as bad wiring, but I always thought Salem had it set."

"Why?"

"Insurance payoff? Who knows? If he didn't need those buildings anymore and he could find a way to make money off them, he would get rid of them however best benefited him. He was a businessman, Deputy."

Dave put his hands on the armrests and pushed himself up.

Celeste put out her hand palm down, as if to be kissed, but he slid his fingers into hers, turned her hand, and shook it firmly.

"I appreciate your time, Mrs. Campbell. And I'm sorry for your loss. Your losses."

"It was nice to meet you, Mr. Hendricks, under bad circumstances."

"Oh, one more thing, ma'am." Dave had planned this for the last thing but acted as if the thought had just occurred to him. He ripped a sheet from his small notebook where he had preprinted the names of their current suspect list:

Tom Jenkins
Burgess Noble
Ron and Denise Rose
Frank White

He leaned over and laid it on the table in front of her. "Are any of these names familiar?"

She read them carefully, holding the paper far out from her as if she was in need of reading glasses but wasn't going to take the time to find them.

"Huh," she said, more a laugh in the back of her throat than a word. "Yes, only one of them."

"Which one is that?"

"I knew a Burgess Noble when I was a teenager."

Now this was a lead. "Knew him how?" Dave prodded.

"We dated, for about six months."

"He's never been in contact with you since?"

She screwed up her face as if the thought of this was outlandish. "No, I heard he left, went to work on the riverboats on the Mississippi, I believe. I don't even know how I knew that."

"What was your time together like?"

"I was sixteen. I thought he was dreamy at the time, but he was too possessive, like most boys at that age. I barely recall it."

This was a remarkable coincidence but at the same time, there wasn't a huge population in this area. Of course people either knew each other or their paths had crossed in the past. Probably nothing, but he'd need to look closer at Noble.

But Celeste spoke again. "The strange thing is, I thought I saw him, just a couple weeks ago. I was leaving here, going to Nashville, and I noticed that a car behind me made every turn I did. Before I got to the Nashville Pike I pulled over on the side of the road to make sure I wasn't being followed, and the car drove past me. The driver looked straight ahead, so I couldn't completely make out his face, but there was something so familiar about him that I obsessed over it a couple days until I finally figured out that he reminded me of Burgess. But I didn't think it was really him. I had the strangest feeling at the time, like I had seen a ghost. I actually wondered to myself if Burgess was still alive after that. And I hadn't thought of him in years. So it maybe *was* him?"

"Well, he just moved back here six months ago, so it's completely possible."

"But why would he be following me?"

"Could be he was just going the same way as you," Dave said, not believing that for a second.

She nodded, more to herself than to agree with him, and her eyes drifted away.

This was strange. Dave would follow up on Burgess, get more history, and see if it led anywhere.

"All right then," Dave said. "I guess that's all for now."

The housekeeper—Carol Ann, he remembered her name was—appeared out of thin air and escorted him back to the front door.

"Have a good day," she said, her voice low, as if she was accustomed to not speaking very loudly in this space.

"Is there anything you'd like to tell me?" he asked before he stepped out the door she had opened for him.

"About what?"

"Anything this past weekend that struck you as strange?"

She glanced down the hallway and then back to him. "No more than usual."

"What does that mean?"

"These are very rich people, Mr. Hendricks. Everything they do is strange to me."

He certainly agreed with her on that, but he didn't want to reveal his alliance on this; he'd keep that card in his back pocket in case he needed to play it later. "Do you travel back and forth with her, to Nashville?"

"No, I take care of this house only. Open it up for them when they're using it, clean it when it stands empty, all of that. I live in the caretaker's cottage out back."

"You have the best view of the lake of any one of us, then."

"I reckon so," she replied. "One reason I took the job."

"You're from here originally?"

"Born and raised. I've known Celeste—Mrs. Campbell—since I was a child. We were both raised on the river."

Dave was surprised by this. "She's from the area?"

"Oh, yeah. She wasn't always so hoity-toity. Grew up poorer than I did. You're probably too young to remember Bonnytown."

"I've heard people talk about it. Little bitty community, wasn't it?"

She nodded.

"Pretty far back in the mountains?"

"So far back the sun didn't come up until noon and went down at three," she said and revealed a mischievous smile. He liked her for that. "Fifty feet under the lake now."

"And you've worked here a long time?"

"Ever since she married Mr. Campbell. Twenty years now. I had moved away for a bit but after I lost my husband, I came back home and I heard she needed the help, so I applied. It's been a mostly easy job," she said, and grinned. "They're in Nashville most of the time."

The working class always had an understanding and it stood in the air between Dave and this lady. He nodded.

"All right, if you think of anything that might help, you can reach me at the marina or leave a message at the sheriff's office."

"I know who you are, Mr. Hendricks. You were the mayor," Carol Ann said, and she didn't have to add what he knew what was in her mind: *the mayor who got drunk and ran his car into the courthouse and resigned in shame.*

"That was me, in another life," he said.

"The older I get, the less judgment I have against anyone," she said, and he was struck by her kindness. He felt they could have been friends in different circumstances. He'd like to sit on the houseboat porch, drink Irish whiskey with her and hear some of her stories about the rich folks' antics. "And having a few different lives is a good thing."

"Well, I thank you for that." He stepped out the door.

"Be careful," she said, the standard farewell of country people, and then added one more traditional send-off in this part of the world: "And watch for deer."

Chapter 18

Sheila was smoking and eating fries and a chili bun from the Dixie Café at the same time. She took a bite, chewed gingerly, swallowed it down, took a draw of her Lucky Strike, then washed it all down with a drink of her cherry Coke.

"Victor is still on the scene, but I have most of what you need to know," she said as soon as Dave sat down across from her desk. "The main thing is that we've got a definite connection even beyond the two deceased being kin."

"A message left at the scene."

"Bingo." She took another bite and talked around the cud of chili, mustard, onions, and bun. "Salem's clothes were folded up real neat on the bank. Dress pants, suit jacket, button-down shirt, tie. All stacked on top of his wingtips. And inside the front pocket on his shirt was a piece of paper with 'Iniquity of the Father' printed on it in ink."

"I was afraid of that," Dave said. "So the killer made Salem strip down as an extra act of humiliation?"

"I guess so," Sheila replied, and picked up the waxed paper cup again for more cherry Coke. "Kept his socks, undershorts, and undershirt on him, though."

"Stabbed?"

"Gutted," Sheila corrected.

"So, taken out into the water and slashed across the gut."

"Maybe. In the preliminary Vashti found no evidence of a struggle and the team found no blood anywhere at the site; they searched the shoreline in a large area."

"That doesn't make a whole lot of sense. Nobody saw anything?"

"That area doesn't get a lot of boaters and is mostly only used by locals who drive, walk in, or ride in on horses," Sheila answered. "By lake the Flatwoods is pretty cut off, with only a little gap providing access to boats, so most people just don't even go up in there."

"But we're certain it happened there, at the Flatwoods?"

Sheila had just put one too many fries into her mouth, so she only nodded for a moment before speaking. "Well, his clothes were folded up there on the bank. But it's possible he could have been brought there."

"Only a local would even *know* about the Flatwoods." He said this aloud, but not for Sheila's benefit since she would have already come to this conclusion herself.

Now she was tapping her finger on the papers before her. "Speaking of locals, we should talk about what these deeds reveal."

Dave grabbed a couple of her fries, dabbed them in the puddle of ketchup on the paper bag and popped them into his mouth, gaining an ill look from Sheila before she went on. They were delicious enough to make him decide he needed to stop in at the Dixie as soon as he left this meeting.

Atlas Boone burst into the room, pecking lightly on the door once he was already in. "How do, Sheila? Dave?"

"Howdy, Atlas," Dave said, turning in his seat. "What do you need?"

Atlas positioned a big smile on his face. He had large teeth that reminded Dave of peppermint Chiclets gum. He had too many teeth and they—combined with his ever-present bright bow ties—made him look goofier than he actually was. "Is Victor about?"

"No, he's still out at the Flatwoods," Sheila offered, "at the murder scene."

"Listen, you tell him: I need for this to go away," he said, and held up the front page of the *Shady Valley Sentinel* between two hands. The headline BRUTAL MURDER ON THE LAKE loomed large there. "And I imagine they're drawing up the new headline today. '*Two* Brutal Murders on the Lake.'"

Dave wanted to ask him exactly how he expected these killings to just go away. Or should the newspaper just not report on it?

"It's the height of tourist season," Atlas said, struggling to keep the smile on his face. He had always been the kind of person who wanted to simultaneously be everyone's boss yet also to be liked by everyone. Things didn't work that way. "And this sure ain't gonna help business."

"What would you suggest, Mayor?" Sheila knew just how to play men like this: make them feel like you cared what they thought when in fact you did not care one bit.

"I would suggest getting it solved yesterday. And to not tell this new reporter one single detail. Have you read this?" He held the newspaper up close to his face and lifted his glasses to read: "And I quote: 'The grisly scene suggests either a crime of extreme passion or a madman on the loose.'" Atlas's smile at last faded and his face was taken over by exasperation. "Grisly! Extreme! *Madman!*" He crumpled the paper and tossed it into the wire wastebasket beside Sheila's desk. "This woman isn't reporting the news, she's writing about it like it's a murder mystery!"

"We don't have any control over the *Sentinel*, Atlas," Dave said, struggling to not sound impatient. He thought Nina had written a pretty compelling, if not completely objective, sentence.

Atlas regained his composure, obviously reminding himself that his philosophy on remaining mayor was to remain affable, yet firm. He straightened his bow tie even though it had not been crooked. There was the Chiclets smile again.

"I was surprised to hear you agreed to be deputized by Victor," Atlas said, "but I'm glad. It's a comfort to know you're on the team, Dave. So I'm asking you to make sure this woman doesn't know anything you don't absolutely have to reveal. And if there are any resources I can offer to make this move faster, please let me know."

"Sounds good, Atlas," Dave said. "I appreciate it."

"Thank you," he said, and nodded. "Good day, Sheila."

"You too, Mayor," Sheila said, and as soon as Atlas spun on his heel to leave, she rolled her eyes at Dave. "*Lord*," she said, and Dave laughed.

"The Tennessee Valley Authority started buying up the land as early as 1935 even though the lake didn't officially open until 1940," Sheila said, getting right back to it. "They were required by law to pay a fair price, so they usually paid more than local rates would have gotten, but this still didn't pacify people who didn't want to leave their land."

Sheila was telling him nothing he didn't already know. He had lived it, as had she. But Sheila was always thorough, even if her social graces weren't the best. A plop of mustard had fallen onto the lapel of her blouse but when Dave put up his finger to point it out, Sheila waved it away, barging forward in her explanation. "So, what I found out right away was that the land where the fishing camp now stands was owned by the McGann family, who moved to Mississippi as soon as they sold out to Campbell a few months before the Corps came in. All the McGann children—all boys—died in the war without ever producing any children, and the parents died shortly thereafter. So that's a dead end," she said, and wiped chili from her mouth. Sheila rarely laughed, but she did occasionally speak a "Ha ha" when something struck her as funny. She did that now. "Ha ha. No pun intended."

"So none of them getting revenge for some slight by Salem Campbell."

"Wait, there's more," Sheila said. "The McGanns owned most of that property, but two other families owned a few acres of it, too."

"And they were?"

"Ten acres of it was owned by a preacher named Waylon Boggs, who tried to sue over it but the lawsuit went nowhere. Salem had every judge around here in his pocket. Seems like Boggs gave up after that. I found out that Boggs and Salem's father had trouble in the past. Back in the early twenties. Boggs raised a stink over that, too, but he eventually dropped it. Became a preacher and seems to have lived pretty quietly. And the final twelve acres of it belonged to the Berry family."

"Steve Berry's father?"

"Actually, his grandfather."

"Strange. That he was at the murder scene this morning. Strange that his daughter would be the one to find the body."

"Maybe the universe is righting itself," Sheila offered, and he was surprised that she would suggest something not deeply rooted in a fact that could be proven.

"But Salem Campbell bought up all kinds of land around what would become the lake," Dave said. "Everybody knows that he snatched up as much as he could before the lake was even announced, including—"

"The land where he built his mansion," Sheila finished for him, and pulled out a large green roster with DEEDS spelled out on its cover in white ink. She had paperclipped the pages she wanted to show him. "Looks like he made sure he got this as soon as he was shown the way the lake would lay. It was the first piece he bought, in 1934. A full year before the government started acquiring land. Had to be right after his first meeting with the Tennessee Valley Authority. Looking at the map I'd say it is definitely the best piece of property in the entire area, view-wise. Looks out on the widest part of the lake."

"Yep, I just saw that view for the first time this morning, when I went to interview Salem's widow."

"I've never even seen that woman in person, as long as she's been married to him," Sheila said. "What's she like?"

"She described herself as a poor little rich girl. I'd say that's about right," Dave said. "She's a pretty woman, really elegant. Seems miserable. She puts on airs, that's for sure. Lots of carefully chosen words and this way of being that makes you think she feels like she's better than anybody else. But if you listen close, you can still hear the Bonnytown in her accent."

"That's why people dislike her so much—she tries to act like something she's not. I heard she was raised poor as Job's turkey."

"Well, she's the opposite now. That view is pretty spectacular. Who'd he con out of that?"

Sheila held her cigarette between the two fingers she used to tap on the blue ink in the ledger, but the writing was too small for him to read it without putting his face close to the page. No matter, since Sheila already knew it by heart.

"Matthew Walker sold it to Salem Campbell for five thousand dollars. Two hundred acres."

"Wow. So that's about—" Dave tried to do the math in his head, but Sheila had already figured it.

"Twenty-five dollars an acre. When the average price for an acre of farmland that rich, with bottomland on the river, was about fifty dollars. And of course Walker had no way to know it would become the most valuable land in the county once the lake came in. The Corps offered abutting landowners sixty-six an acre."

"So he completely did him wrong."

"He screwed him," Sheila said, putting it more the way one of his army buddies would have, "and didn't even kiss him."

"Whoa, Sheila," Dave said, laughing.

"Walker relocated to eastern Kentucky, where he was from originally, but it looks like one daughter of his married local. She moved away shortly before the lake was opened." Sheila began to shuffle through the other papers. "I had her name here, just a second."

"Her name was Elizabeth Walker, and she married James Owens," Dave said.

Sheila stopped looking through the papers. "How do you know that?"

"They're Nina Owens's parents."

"Nina?" Sheila asked. "The new reporter at the *Sentinel*?"

Dave only nodded.

"Atlas's new archenemy. Something I don't like about her," Sheila said, and lit another cigarette. "Something I don't trust. Too much sass." Her first exhalation seemed loud in the silence between them.

"Sass?"

"Yeah. Too perky. Like she always knows more than everybody else and is too pleased with herself about it. I don't like that."

Dave had never known of Sheila to like any woman, but he had to admit he understood what she meant about Nina. Still, the very thing Sheila found annoying about Nina was what charmed him. The mystery about her was both appealing and frustrating. That mystery caused him to not be able to quite trust her but had also been one reason he'd been unable to resist her.

"So we have two murders and at both are descendants of people who were cheated out of fair prices," Dave said, not even sure why he was saying it aloud.

"Nina was with you at Esau's murder scene, and Steve Berry was present at Salem's."

"Right."

Sheila popped the last bite of her chili bun into her mouth and swallowed it down. "Well, there are only so many families in this place," she said. "It's not so far-fetched. It's a coincidence."

"Well," Dave said, "I don't believe in coincidences. Maybe one, but not two."

"So one of them could be our killer?"

"If we're going with the theory that this is some kind of crazy revenge plot, then they sure could be. There are lots of people whose family land was taken by Salem," Dave said. "But only these two were also at the scenes."

"So they for sure go on the chalkboard. Steve Berry and Nina Owens." Sheila sounded especially satisfied that she could add Nina to the bunch.

Now all Dave had to do was make sure no one knew he had slept with one of them last night. He felt a momentary return of his hangover stomach at the thought that he might have compromised the case in some way by getting drunk last night and falling into bed with Nina, only two days after they had reconnected. What had he been thinking? He had not been thinking at all, that's what. There was definitely motive, but did he really believe Nina was capable of something like this? He didn't want to think so—more than anything she was his friend, and old friendships like that meant something—but if he knew one thing to be true, it's that most people are capable of far more than we ever give them credit for. He had learned a long time ago to never be too surprised by anything or anybody.

"We need to pull the deeds to see if Salem also owned the land that abuts the Flatwoods."

"Way ahead of you," Sheila said, and pulled out another ledger from her stack, this one with a red cover. "The Berrys still own all that land that runs down to the shoreline—"

"Which the Corps of Engineers owns," Dave said. Everyone knew this. "That'd make sense. The Berrys live at the top of the mountain just up from the Flatwoods.

I guess their family has owned that land since it was parceled out after the Revolutionary War."

"These records only go back to 1850—the courthouse burned back then, so that's as far back as we can go with any of these deeds—and the Berrys owned it then," Sheila said. "So I'm betting you're right."

"This is all good to know," Dave said, standing. "Hey, I need you to track down Burgess Noble and get him to come into the station for a follow up."

"All I can do is send somebody out there. No phone lines out in that part of the county."

"Find somebody to take him a message to come in, then," Dave said. "Soon as possible."

"You got some kind of lead on him?"

"Well, Salem Campbell's widow dated him in high school."

"That's a lead."

"Maybe. Maybe not. The bigger thing for me is that she thinks he may have been following her a couple weeks ago."

Sheila pulled a face to suggest that this sounded like a real lead to her, and nodded. "I'll get him in here. Tomorrow morning?"

"Sounds good," Dave said.

The phone rang sharply and Sheila snatched it up. As she talked behind him, Dave looked out the long, wide window on the town. Down below was the Confederate memorial, a white concrete cupola with Stonewall Jackson standing atop it, holding his hat rested against his right leg and a saber posed against his left one. He gazed southward, pining for the past. Meanwhile, a huge crow had settled on his head and was surveying the town along with Dave. Shoppers moved in and out of the stores and cars crawled along the state line straddling Main Street. Somewhere out there a murderer was lurking. More than that: a madman, just as Nina had written. Or maybe even a madwoman, as unlikely as it might seem.

Behind him he heard Sheila settle the phone back on its cradle. "That was Jimmy Storms," she said. "He interviewed Patricia Campbell at her dormitory."

"Anything worth reporting?"

"Not much. She never really knew her half-brother, so she couldn't offer much information. Jimmy says she seemed ashamed of how wealthy her family is but didn't seem to have any hatred for her father. Jimmy offered her police protection, like Victor suggested, but she refused it. She said it was hard enough to go to school there as a politician's daughter and she sure didn't want security following her around."

"Did he inform her about her father?"

"He was already beyond the range of the police radio by the time he was found, so Jimmy didn't even know about it yet when he was with her; I just told him."

"Now that two members of her family are dead, I'd say Victor will be demanding she take that protection."

"We'll see," Sheila said, sounding doubtful.

"You don't think so?"

"I think Victor is pretty overwhelmed right now. I'm glad you're here."

Dave was embarrassed to be complimented. "Well, you've made me hungry, so I'm off to the Dixie."

Sheila had already turned to her typewriter and was pecking away with a fresh Lucky Strike between her teeth. She didn't respond when he told her good-bye. She never did.

Chapter 19

Two o'clock was the least busy time of day to be in the Dixie Café. There was only one other table occupied when Dave entered—four teenagers sharing a milkshake with four straws and giggling like this was the funniest thing they'd ever done. Fats Domino was singing "Ain't That a Shame" on the jukebox and they were moving their shoulders around to the music. A small sign on a silver pole instructed him to seat himself, so he did so.

As soon as he sat down he saw that Steve Berry was in the kitchen, so he figured he might as well feel him out a bit while he was here.

Steve's back was to him, and Dave could make out the figure of a young woman who appeared from the rear of the kitchen. Immediately Steve moved toward her, throwing his arms in the air in front of him. She flinched in a way that made Dave feel like she had been in this situation before. She wasn't close enough for him to recognize, but he could tell she was at least a decade younger than either himself or Steve. Dave couldn't hear anything, but it was clear by Steve's body language that he was chewing her out, and after just a moment the woman ran away, presumably to the back of the kitchen. Steve followed, disappearing behind the kitchen wall.

Steve had been a couple of years ahead of him in school, not exactly quiet but he was unassuming and never inserted himself into a conversation unless invited. He was known around town as someone who worked hard. The Dixie was meticulously clean and the orders always came out accurately, mostly because Steve was always there. Dave would have been surprised for anyone else to be working after what he had gone through this morning, but not Steve. He was practically always at the Dixie since he had taken it over from his father, who had run it when Dave was growing up.

Steve had stepped in shortly after graduating from high school and this had been his life ever since, an honest living that he seemed happy to have taken on. Steve seemed to thrive on the incredible busyness the café experienced in spurts and the calms between. He was the kind of owner/manager who was completely hands-on, so much that it wasn't unusual for him to sometimes come out to your table and take your order himself, as he was on his way to do right now for Dave.

Apparently Steve was a good actor because the anger Dave had witnessed in the man only a minute before was not evident as he plucked a yellow pencil from behind his ear and held a small green pad in front of him. He gave a wide smile, completely relaxed after a day of interacting with a dead body and an argument with a girl in his kitchen. "How do, Dave?"

"I'm doing very well, Steve. How about you?"

"Fair to middling," Steve said, which was how he always answered this question, as did most people in this section of Kentucky and Tennessee. Now that Dave looked at him closeup, he could see that beyond the smile and faked state of ease Steve was hollow-eyed and pale, dark shadows around his eyes as if he hadn't slept well for the past week.

"Heard y'all had a big scare," Dave said. "I'm working with the sheriff on the case."

"The worst part was how bad it tore up Lily," he said. "I'm afraid she'll never get over it."

"Kids have a way of healing up way quicker than we do, I reckon," Dave said. This sounded like the right thing to say.

"I hope so. I hated to see her so afraid." He fretted his brow and it was clear to Dave that a lot was going on with this man, although he was good at hiding it. Steve shifted on his feet as if physically changing the subject. "Get you something to eat today?"

Dave ordered the chili bun with mustard and onions, medium fries, and a large cherry Coke. He had been craving all three since witnessing Sheila devour hers.

"All right, that'll only take a minute or two," Steve said, and gave a little nod before spinning on one heel and padding back to the kitchen. As Steve walked away, Dave wondered if the argument had been a simple interaction between a good boss and an employee who had messed up somehow, or was there a bigger trouble going on here? There had been something in that moment when he flailed his arms at the woman that made it seem more like a couple getting into it than a disagreement between a boss and employee.

The Dixie Café was one of those little restaurants that every small town in the South possessed. Booths made of rich maple tables and red leather benches, a scattering of white Formica tables with silver chairs outfitted with red leather seats and backs, a bright jukebox, the walls covered with photos of townspeople from the last one hundred years, all in cheap gold frames. A menu with only ten items, but all of them delicious.

Now LaVern Baker was singing "Tweedle Dee" on the jukebox and the teenagers were all singing along and laughing; they knew every word. All four of their heads turned when the door opened and Nina rushed in. She was wearing a full white skirt and a matching tight blouse along with a little red scarf tied loosely at her neck, with the knot to the side. He knew this was the style but couldn't help wondering if it was there to cover up a hickey he might have left.

Nina went straight to the counter—obviously getting something to go—and saw Dave only after the young woman had emerged from the back and taken her order. She gave a little wave and hurried over to him.

"Hey there, handsome," she said, which made him uncomfortable. Last night should not have happened; it was too soon and he barely knew this woman, even if he had known her so well twenty-five years ago. He felt embarrassed that only twelve hours ago they had been all tangled up, naked, and now she was being so casual about it all. He'd never done anything like this before and he felt stupid somehow. Plus he felt bad about drinking two nights in a row. Not to mention that she was now on the suspect list, no matter how thin the connection. So far.

"What are you up to today?" Dave asked.

"I just came from the Flatwoods."

"Did Victor let you on the scene?"

"No," she said, her demeanor changing once she realized Dave hadn't offered for her to sit down. But he had thought she was in a hurry by the way she had sailed in.

"You want to sit down a minute?"

"No, I have to get to the office," she said. She glanced over at the teenagers, who were watching them as if they expected something to happen. She gave them a hard look and they turned away. "They need this piece before typesetting starts at five."

"So you did get something for your story, then."

"Not really. Victor sent Zeke out with the particulars they were going to share. Just where the body was found, and by who. No cause of death or anything specific. Now that the family's notified they're going to let me run that it was Salem Campbell, so that alone makes for a big story. My piece will basically have three lines of real information and then a glorified obit."

Dave only nodded.

"You okay?" she asked, and lowered her head, squinting one eye at him.

"Why sure," he said, and smiled unconvincingly.

"I know it was too soon," she said, sweeping her auburn hair off her forehead. "But you only live once, you know? I think we're all too uptight about sex."

Dave couldn't help but to look around to make sure the teenagers hadn't heard her use this word.

She gave a little laugh but didn't acknowledge his nervousness otherwise. "Let's not let it ruin our friendship, okay?"

"It won't," he said. "Don't worry."

The young woman held up a brown paper bag at the counter and said, "Food's up, ma'am!" Dave definitely didn't know her; he was sure he had never seen her before.

Nina gave her a nod and turned back to Dave. "Want to give me a quote about Frank? The whole town knows y'all have him in jail, so you might as well give them something to keep the gossip down."

"I'm not at liberty to do that. You should contact Victor about—"

"Already did. I'll say one thing for ole Victor, he's good at stonewalling."

"It's an important part of the job."

"Well, I'll see you tonight," Nina said, then grinned. "Unless you want to feed me any juicy details about the Salem Campbell murder before I go."

"Wish I could," he said. "But I doubt Victor let you know it was murder, so you best not run that."

"Doesn't take a genius to figure it out. His son killed one day, him dead the next. I've kept that 'sins of the father' stuff out of the paper, but that doesn't mean I've wiped it from my mind." Before he could say more, she pranced away. "Don't worry," she called over her shoulder, plucked up her food, and she was gone.

Steve brought his food and drink back on a cork tray, which he sat down on the table. Dave immediately grabbed a fry but spoke before Steve could turn and leave.

"Like I said, I'm a deputy now—"

"Yeah, I heard y'all had arrested some coal miner who was staying at the fishing camp," Steve interrupted.

Dave only nodded to that. "Got time for me to ask you a couple questions?"

Steve pulled a chair out and sat down. "Not exactly rush hour," he said. He sat with both elbows on the table, hunched over. "I had planned to take the day off to go fishing but after what happened, I just came on in, once Lily got calmed down. I never take off work and then this happens."

Dave bit into the chili bun and savored it a moment. He hadn't realized how famished he was until the food was before him. He thought he'd take a different approach with this interview and let Steve do the leading on his own. "You've been told who the victim was?"

Steve nodded, not looking Dave in the eye.

"Anything at all you noticed that might be of interest to us?"

Steve shook his head. "Nothing much to tell. Lily was bound and determined to swim even though I didn't want her to. Somehow it just doesn't seem fitting to swim in the morning. But she was so excited, we decided to let her go in for a minute. Now I doubt she'll ever go back in."

"We?"

"Susan was with us."

Dave hadn't been told Steve's wife was there.

Steve went on. "That made it even worse, of course."

"Why do you say that?" Dave asked.

"Well, she's six months pregnant. That kind of shock can't be good for the baby."

"Did you realize who it was right away?" Dave ate another fry; this whole eating while interviewing made it all seem a lot more casual. Might be a good tactic.

"I barely glanced at that body. I grabbed Lily, jumped in the truck, and we got the hell out of there. Drove back down to the house and called the sheriff's office. It was a couple hours later before Zeke Collins came and told me who it was. He said he wasn't supposed to."

"That sounds like Zeke."

"But he did say to keep it quiet until they told the family."

"That was good of him," Dave scoffed. "And what'd you think, when you found out it was Salem Campbell?"

"Honestly?" Steve said. "I was relieved it was him and not somebody who didn't deserve it."

Dave did a good job of hiding his surprise, he thought, at hearing Steve say something like this. Not because most people wouldn't have felt similarly but because Steve was normally so mild-mannered.

"I know that sounds bad, but Salem messed over my family back in the thirties. He messed over lots of families." Anger was rising in Steve's face, his eyes narrowing. "Took the land for half what he knew it'd be worth. I grew up hearing those stories."

"Me too," Dave said.

"Then you know about what he did at Ghost Island."

The lake ran the length of a wide area, covering about fifty square miles, so it wasn't unusual for there to be whole sections that some people had intimate knowledge of and others didn't. Ghost Island was about as far away from the area where Dave had grown up as anyplace on the lake. He knew it mostly as the place that had the most sought-after camping on the lake, and one made even more popular by the legend that it was haunted. Thus its name.

"No, I don't."

"The Bethel Cemetery was there and the people fought every way they could for those graves to not be disturbed. Took it to the court and even held up the lake construction for a year."

"The Corps of Engineers had to move all the graves, though," Dave offered. "They couldn't have caskets washing up on the lake banks."

"But that's the thing," Steve said, talking faster now, as if desperate to get it all out. "That's high land. That graveyard was atop the mountain. It was high enough elevation that the graveyard could have been left alone and even though it became an island, the families that had dead buried there could still have taken boats over to decorate the graves and such. But the Corps of Engineers knew it was a prime place for boat-in camping, and they wanted it as a showcase for tourists. So Salem did some kind of behind the scenes shenanigans that got approval from the capital to move all those graves. They had writs on all of it. They could've been left alone, but somebody in the Corps slipped Salem some money and he did their dirty work."

"Is there any proof of that, though?"

"No. But everybody knew it at the time. Salem even bragged about it, later."

"That's terrible," Dave said.

"Even more terrible if it's your great-grandparents and all of your dead ancestors being dug up so that damned old bastard could make more money, even though he has more than he could ever spend anyway. And maybe even worse is that they say they didn't get all the bodies. Sometimes they just took the headstones to make it look like no grave was there, to make it all quicker and easier," Steve said, and suddenly got up. His chair made such a loud scrape that the teenagers turned their faces toward Dave and Steve. "So it might sound ill-mannered of me, but I don't mind one damn bit that he's dead. I hate for anybody to die. Especially to get murdered. But good riddance."

Dave tried to not show any reaction at all, hoping Steve would keep going with this line of thought. Dave was always happy to be quiet and let people reveal everything they possibly could about themselves.

"Sorry to lose my temper," Steve said, and leaned both hands on the red chair. "That kind of injustice just burns me up."

"I understand, Steve," Dave said, and this was true. This was certainly more emotion than he had ever seen Steve Berry put on display, but he still had gone about it more calmly than Dave would have if his family's graves had been so unnecessarily disturbed. "I hope Lily's feeling better. She will, soon."

Steve nodded. "I sure hope so," he said, and turned, trudging away like a man carrying a heavy load.

After he paid his bill, Dave strolled back out into the afternoon heat. Instead of going back to his car, which was parked at the sheriff's office, Dave hurried down the street and eased into an alley where he could see the back door of the Dixie Café. He leaned close against the wall so he was out of sight. The young woman was out there on a concrete stoop, solemnly smoking a cigarette. After a moment, Steve came out, did a quick sweep of the street with his eyes to see if anyone was nearby, then leaned in for a quick kiss on the lips. Dave might not have known the woman, but he did know for sure she wasn't Steve's pregnant wife.

Chapter 20

Dave hoofed it back up the hill to where his car was parked near the sheriff's office and saw Vashti Bryant parallel parking in the space behind him. He loved her car: a convertible 1953 Buick Skylark, painted blue as a robin's egg, with a stark white interior. If Hitchcock would ever feature a black woman in one of his films—doubtful, Dave knew—she would have fit right in. She was wearing a bright green headscarf and large, white, cat-eye sunglasses. Vashti had slid into the space like a pro and now he couldn't help but notice how beautifully her dress fit her behind as she got out of the car and leaned in to lift her purse from the seat. He had just brought his eyes up when she turned and caught sight of him.

"Take a picture," she said, but before true embarrassment could take him over, she laughed.

"You'd make a mighty pretty one," he said.

"Aw, shucks, Dave. Flattery will get you everywhere." She pulled the sunglasses down on her nose just enough for him to see seriousness in her eyes. "Not really."

He laughed. "You know I like you for your brains more than anything else."

"I hope so," she said. "I *guess*." Vashti untied the headscarf and tucked it into her purse, then snapped the bag shut with a sharp click. "What are you up to?"

"No good, as usual," he said.

Vashti began to walk toward the courthouse so he fell in line with her, passing his car, but choosing to be with her as long as he could. "And the investigation?"

"We're making lots of connections. Sheila Shepherd is the best partner anybody could have on a case like this."

"She's the smartest woman I've ever known," Vashti said.

"And you're the only woman I've ever known her to respect."

"Well, I have to say, with Sheila that really means something."

Dave put two fingers on Vashti's wrist and she stopped for a moment, pausing and looking down, but then she pulled away, not unkindly.

"How about we have a nice supper at Dot's when I get this case sewn up?"

"Dave, you know that's not possible. Flirting is fun, but it's just—" she stopped, either searching for the right word or hesitating to say it. He bet on the latter.

"What?"

"A fantasy."

"Haven't you figured out by now that I don't care what anyone thinks?"

"Not even the Klan? Not even the anti-miscegenation laws?" Vashti began walking again, quicker this time. He hastened to keep up. "Listen, it might be a game to you, but for me it's real life. I don't need the trouble, no matter how handsome and charming you are."

"I'm not talking about getting married," he started.

"That's a comfort," she interrupted. "Just what every girl wants to hear."

"You know what I mean. I'm talking about dinner. Some drinks. A nice time together."

Vashti's heels made smart clicks on the stone steps of the courthouse. She stopped at the door, her hand on the brass handle. "How are we going to have a dinner date at Dot's? You ever seen a black person at Dot's before?" She searched his face but didn't give him time to answer. "No? Because they won't seat us."

"Dot wouldn't refuse any—"

Vashti shook her head and issued a heavy sigh. "Believe me, she would. And the fact that you don't understand that is reason enough for us to only be friends. So quit asking me out. It just reminds me of how backward this country is. And it's worse because I like you."

He felt the cold sweat of embarrassment washing over him. "I'm so sorry, Vashti. You're right, I should've thought it through more."

"I have to go, Dave. Take good care of yourself." Then she was gone, the door closing softly behind her before he could say more.

Chapter 21

By the time Dave got back to the marina, the heat was casting a gauzy mist over the trees in the distance. Boats zipped back and forth across the big water between the Marie and the fishing camp across the way, the water dotted by swimmers and skiers. At the row of houseboats, several people sat on their porches or floated on innertubes. Elvis Presley was singing out to those in the water from a loud radio.

Dave could have used a dip himself but he had work to do, work he had been putting off, and Rex had already been plenty patient with him. Rex had five johnboats he rented out to folks, and all but one of them had been returned this morning. They needed a good cleaning since they hadn't been washed down in a while. He'd also fill up the gas tanks, make sure the life vests weren't moldy, and check all the ropes. When he reached the little corral of boats bobbing gently on the green water, he saw the one he had borrowed from the Capability Fishing Camp and remembered that he still hadn't returned it. There was no real rush, he reckoned, since Celeste Campbell had closed the camp down for the time being. Made sense, he thought. Probably not a lot of people lining up to come spend a few days where a brutal murder had just occurred. Some workman would have to apply a few layers of paint to cover up that red writing on the wall.

Dave had just soaped down the first boat when he saw Jesse Monahan, the water patrolman for the Kentucky side, easing over the water toward him in his runabout. The boat was turquoise and white with a fiberglass hut over the steering wheel that was topped by a large blue light, with the Kentucky state seal emblazoned on the right side. Jesse waved and smiled when Dave looked up. Dave envied Jesse his job of cruising around the lake all day, issuing an occasional citation for a fishing violation or not having the required safety items on board. Most of the time Jesse was able to anchor down and laze beneath the shade while he watched for boaters to do something wrong through his binoculars. He was a nice fellow, easygoing and always smiling, so Dave couldn't begrudge him his gravy job too much. Jesse had been a state trooper for many years and had probably earned it. He was a slender old man with the kind of white hair that Dave imagined looked better on him than whatever his original color had been. He was tanned a deep bronze from his hours out on the lake, and the crow's feet at his eyes made his smile seem somehow wider. Only when Jesse got closer could Dave see that the water patrol boat was towing an empty wooden rowboat behind it.

"How do, Dave?" Jesse called as he cut the motor a few feet out from the dock so they could talk easily.

"How do." Dave nodded and unbent himself from his scrubbing, his back giving a pleasing pop as he did so.

"Y'all missing a boat? Found this one adrift up in Catfish Cove."

"Not one of ours, Jesse."

"Strange thing is it looks like somebody tried to sink it," Jesse said. As he drew closer, Dave could see a large hole had been knocked in the front right side. Whoever had done it had made the opening too high, though, not realizing the hole would be mostly above water when the boat was afloat. *So they damaged it while it was pulled up on shore*, Dave thought. "I've gone around to every occupied campsite on the lake, and nobody's claiming it. And it doesn't belong to any of the fishing camps."

The boat was old but in sturdy shape except for the intentional damage.

"What do you reckon Rex would think about me mooring it here until someone claims it?" Jesse asked. "I'm betting someone would come here inquiring before anywhere else, and since we don't have a station on the lake, it's the only place I could think of."

"He won't mind a bit," Dave offered, knowing Rex would be the first to allow Jesse anything he needed.

"Alrighty," Jesse said. "I'll bring it on in if you'll catch me."

Jesse pulled his runabout into the dock expertly and left his motor idling while Dave untied the rope from the silver hook on the back and tossed it into him. He bent to secure it to the dock and saw that the floor was full of mud and rocks.

"Heard you were working for Victor," Jesse said, a little disbelief tinging his words.

restoring order. Even beyond that, he liked the feeling the constant repetition of scrubbing gave to the muscles in the lower part of his back and his shoulders. He liked seeing something that had been dirty become clean, as if seeing something righted before his eyes. He whistled some Jimmie Rodgers, pushing air pleasingly between his lips. He was trying to give himself a break from the murders, but the gears in his mind were running wild.

He kept thinking about the fact that both Nina and Steve Berry were connected to the deeds of land that were important to Salem Campbell. He kept thinking about how they had both been present at scenes of crimes, seemingly by coincidence. He kept thinking how he didn't believe in coincidence.

Dave also studied on how Nina had showed up so late that night on the boat beside him. He needed to know where she had been, and if she could prove it. His mind was running wild with every possibility, and one of them was that she could have easily done the crime at the Capability Fishing Camp, crossed the lake in the rowboat a few coves up from the Marie, tried to sink the boat, then climbed up to the road and walked to wherever she had left her car on the side of the road down to the marina, then shown up at her own houseboat at three in the morning as if nothing had happened, knowing Dave would be a solid alibi. The others had been playing cards with Esau until half past two, and Vashti thought Esau had been killed shortly thereafter, so it would have been tight, but Nina could have done it. He couldn't know for sure without a reenactment but as he ran it through his mind, it seemed

"Working *with* him," Dave said. "Just helping out with the investigations."

"Terrible stuff," Jesse said. He was running his forefinger into the bottom of a pouch of Red Man chewing tobacco. "I know Esau had a bad reputation, but he was always friendly to me."

"You know about the other one?" Dave said, careful to not reveal too much, even to a fellow lawman.

"I heard, yeah," Jesse said, and popped a plug of the tobacco into the space between his teeth and his right jaw. "Won't be too many mourners lined up for old Salem, I'd say. Sad, really, that a man with everything like him would waste his whole life treating people poorly."

"That's the truth," Dave said.

"Well, I reckon I should be getting on," Jesse said, and popped the boat into gear. "Lots of folks out on the lake and they need looking after." He threw a hand into the air. "I'll check back in a day or two and see if the boat was claimed."

"Looks to me like somebody was trying to get shed of it," Dave said.

"I thought the same," Jesse agreed, "but whoever damaged it may not be the person who owned it. They might be looking for it."

"Good point," Dave said. "Have a good day, Jesse." Dave stood with his hands on his hips until the water patrolman had turned and put his eyes on the lake.

As much as Dave liked investigating and interrogating, there was something pleasing about manual labor, too. The acts of washing down the boats and figuring out the identity of a murderer were not that different: both were about possible. He didn't want to think this about Nina, especially after what had happened between them last night, but now that he had made that misstep, he had to make up for it by following every possible thought.

Nina having something to do with the boat seemed more likely than Steve, since it wouldn't have made much sense for him to take his daughter swimming where he had dumped the body. Besides, he lived too far down the lake for the boat to have drifted back from where he might have come, and certainly made more sense than anyone at the fishing camp needing it. They had a wealth of rental boats at their disposal they could have eased back in with the others. Especially since the only person who might have noticed—Esau—would have not been present to do a boat count anyway.

He was so deep in thought that he jumped when he heard a deep crash of thunder across the lake. He looked up and saw greenish clouds taking over the sky above him. Instantly the world cooled, shifted as if suddenly unleveled by the approaching summer storm. He looked across the lake and could see the rain heading toward him, shifting like curtains as it made its way over the water.

Dave scampered along the wooden boards and reached the office just as the rain hit the marina. Rex was sitting at his battered desk, a teacup to his mouth.

"Yorkshire in the pot," he said. "Your favorite. And I made shortbread."

The rain made a pleasing music on the tin roof of the office. Lightning flashed outside and shuddered into the room.

"I think my favorite thing about the South is a summer storm," Rex said. "They're so wild and violent. In England our rain is quiet and dull. Here it's so dramatic. I've been in America over forty years and I still can't get over it."

Dave poured himself a cup of the tea and savored its pleasing bitterness. He chomped into a rectangle of shortbread that emphasized the taste and immediately felt the little jolt that tea-time always gave to him; no wonder the British were such a hardy people. He never could understand why Americans hadn't taken to tea the same way the Brits had.

"I can always count you to keep my confidence, can't I?" Dave said.

"You're the only person I really talk to, lad," Rex said. "Of course you can."

"I found out today that Nina's family had been cheated out of a lot of money twenty years ago by Salem Campbell, and she happened to be with me when we found Esau. And I found out that Steve Berry's family was cheated by Salem, too—"

"And he was at the scene when Salem was found," Rex said, then took another drink of tea as if he needed help in considering all of this.

"Awfully big coincidences, don't you think?"

"Ah well," Rex said, "the thing is, it'd be hard to swing a cat around this entire area without hitting someone whose family wouldn't say Salem was corrupt in some way."

"People do have that opinion. But when you get right down to it, not so many who have hard evidence of that. Sheila produced deeds from the thirties that show

how he bought up their land while withholding knowledge from them that he knew would make those properties skyrocket."

"The building of the lake," Rex said. "He knew earlier than others."

"*Months* before others. And used it to make money for himself."

Outside the storm was already calming. The rain pecked gently at the tin roof now. Dave thought how he maybe should have caught a quick nap instead of stopping in for tea. That sound on the roof and the cool air coming in off the lake after the storm would have been perfection. But now it was another dramatic summer storm coming to its quick close.

"That certainly is a bad neighbor," Rex said. "But it's not surprising."

"Not at all," Dave said. He could feel the tea easing out over his upper torso, relaxing his muscles. "I just can't help putting together the messages left at the scenes and the fact that two people close to the case have histories with him."

"So where does that leave the lad you lot are keeping in jail, then?"

"Trouble is he's already shown he will run. But we won't be able to keep him more than forty-eight hours without any more evidence, and that's about up."

"What's your gut tell you about him?" Rex asked.

"My gut tells me he's a man in real trouble, but I don't know if any of that matters to this specific case. The running makes him look guilty but once you start looking at the suspects, you can find something about each one of them that might raise eyebrows."

"I've always gone on the simplest thought: if it looks like a duck and quacks like a duck—"

"What I've learned in policework is that it's not always a duck, though," Dave said. He had finished his tea and shortbread. Sunlight was flooding through the windows again and the rain had moved away over the Cumberland Plateau. "I need to get away from the case and everything else for a bit. Fancy going out fishing with me once I finish these boats?"

Rex held up a copy of *New Seeds of Contemplation*. "As long as I can take this with me. I was planning on finishing it this afternoon."

"Sounds good," Dave said, and glanced at his watch. "Let's head out around seven and we'll hit the cool part of the evening before dark."

"I'll be ready," Rex said.

★ ★ ★

Dave had just finished a supper of canned tomato soup and a grilled cheese when he heard a heavy knock on his houseboat door. He opened it to find the least expected person possible: Janet, his ex-wife. Now Victor's wife. She had taken a step back from the door and was standing there with her arms crossed, a small black purse clutched to her chest with her right hand. She was wearing a deep green dress that made her black hair darker and brought out the shine in her pretty eyes, which were a deep brown. He hated how he still thought her so beautiful after all of these years. But she was as icy as ever, her face lovely but still a tombstone absent of humor or sweetness.

"What do you want?" he said.

"I want to know what the hell you're up to," she said. "Is this some kind of joke?"

"I don't know what you're talking about."

"Working with Victor. If you're trying to spite me—"

His laughter stopped her from going on. "You never change, do you, Janet? Thinking you're the center of the universe. I hadn't even thought about you in this situation. Not once," he said, knowing there was nothing more horrifying for her to hear.

"Then *why*? To prove some kind of point?"

"Because my community needs me."

"If you hurt him," she said. "If you're doing this just to mess with him, I'll never forgive you."

"That's fine with me. I'm never going to forgive either one of you for what you did to me, sneaking around behind my back. I didn't deserve it, and you know it."

Only now did she take her eyes from his face. "No, you didn't," she said quietly.

He could hardly believe it; she had never offered any kind of remorse at all. Still, he wasn't swayed by this momentary lapse in her hard, cold exterior.

"We both know Victor is a good man," she said. "I'm sorry, Dave, but I love him. And every day of my life I'm worrying about how much he regrets being with me. Because he's not been fully happy since he lost you in his life. You know that, don't you?"

"Do you really think I care, Janet? I don't." He wished he didn't. But his friendship with Victor had always been stronger than his marriage to Janet. He was glad to hear that Janet now lived her life in fear, even if he couldn't bring himself to be delighted to hear that Victor hadn't been happy since.

Janet couldn't focus on another human being too long before going back to herself, though. "How do you think it is for me," she said, "knowing that the worst thing he ever did was fall in love with me?"

"I don't give a flying fuck how it is for you, Janet. Or him." He stepped out onto the porch of the houseboat, causing her to scramble onto the dock to put some space between them. "Get the hell out of here and don't ever come back."

"Just don't be mean to him," she said. "That's all I'm asking of you."

Dave stood on the porch, watching her strut away until she was out of sight.

Chapter 22

Dave's favorite time to be on the water was in the evenings after the boaters had all gone back to their campsites or homes for supper. The waves they had stirred up all day long stilled, leaving the lake to be flat and smooth as a pane of green glass. Dave hated to disturb it as he steered the engine of the boat with Shorty in his lap, her silky ears billowing behind her and her eyes closed against the wind as if in satisfaction. Herons waded white and silent in the shady coves, patiently watching the water and occasionally dipping their necks to scoop up a passing minnow. Turtles lazed on half-submerged logs. The fresh, clean smell of the lake washed against their faces as they drove across the lake.

They eased their johnboat up into a fishing hole known as the Sungranny Spot, named for an especially colorful kind of bluegill that were rumored to love the underwater plant life and conditions of this particular hollow. This was a place that only local fishermen knew and Dave liked it not only because the bites were plentiful but also because it was a peaceful spot, far off the main lake, where the air always seemed to be ten degrees cooler. Pines and cedars stood straight on the steep banks, along with sturdy oaks and tulip poplars that dropped their blooms onto the water in early summer.

This evening a thin mist was easing out of the small creek at the head of the hollow and they could hear the gurgle of the little falls up there. They barely spoke after they baited their hooks, cast out, and waited for a fish to strike. Rex was holding his fishing rod and reading the Merton book. Shorty had curled up on an orange life vest on the floor and gone promptly to sleep, issuing an occasional grunt of contentment. Dave was slowly reeling in his line and waiting for that jolt of excitement he would feel in his arm when a fish tapped on his bait. While he did, he took a long look at the mountainsides around him. The dark brown, wet rocks along the waterline. The red clutches of wild columbines that were growing in the shade of the cedars. His people had roamed these hills, farmed them and loved them for generations. Despite how well he knew this place, there were still times when he had trouble orienting himself to the world before the lake. He thought about where the Sungranny Spot would have been before this particular hollow was flooded. A few miles from where he had grown up. Back then this had been a wild place, barely populated because of its steepness. Most likely a place best known by moonshiners who planted stills here or wildcrafters who dug up ginseng and bloodroot.

It was good to have a friend like Rex, who could be quiet and didn't mind you being quiet, either. Those friends were hard to find. Most people had to fill up every empty space, whether with meaningless blather or materials they didn't need.

That made him think about how simple and spartan Esau's little cottage had been. His lack of possessions did not seem to be a sign of poverty so much as choice; Dave knew plenty of poor people whose houses were crowded with useless knick-knacks and just too many *things*, period. He chided himself for thinking back to the case, but at the same time he found himself mentally moving through Esau's cottage, standing in the shower house, even imagining the folded clothes on the lake bank even though he hadn't been at that crime scene. He knew the Flatwoods well enough to picture it all vividly.

Then there was a jerk at the end of his line and he pulled the rod back with both hands, firmly setting the hook in the translucent lip of the fish. Shorty immediately jumped to her feet and yipped a couple of barks before Dave assured her everything was okay. He reeled it in quick but steady, a little thrill rolling through him when he saw the large bluegill sailing through the clear water beside the boat, pulled forward by his taunt fishing line. He pulled up the fish and held it in his right hand while he removed the hook. The bluegill was fat and beautiful, its forehead a glowing golden-orange.

"Look at that," he said, and held it out to Rex.

"That'll fry up nice," Rex said.

But as the fish's blood-red gills gasped for air in his hand, Dave thought about how he'd have to clean it. The slice down its middle, the bluish-purple guts plucked out, its large eye watching the entire time. He couldn't help thinking of the slice across Esau's side. He wondered if that had been accidental—just another coincidence that a man who ran a fishing camp had been cut so similarly to a gutted fish—or if there was something more there.

He dropped it back into the water, pleased by the sound it made when it broke the surface and zoomed away. The sound of freedom.

Chapter 23

All the way back to the Marie, Dave thought about the drifting boat. He hadn't thought too much about it when Jesse Monahan had brought it to the dock, but now he couldn't get it out of his mind. Empty boats floating about the lake weren't unheard of but they were certainly uncommon, and they were almost always claimed quickly. Sometimes someone didn't tie them up properly at a campsite or the dock, sometimes a storm jostled them loose. It didn't make any sense that Jesse had checked with all the campers yet none of them reported a boat missing. And it being damaged on purpose made it seem even more suspicious. Besides, he had to consider that every single thing might be part of the Campbell murders. An unmoored boat with a hole in its side floating about Cedar Lake during the same time as two murders was something else that seemed like a coincidence. And Dave did not trust coincidences.

When they came around the bend at the mouth of Catfish Cove, Dave slowed and cut the engine.

"Something wrong?"

"Just need to talk a minute," Dave said. The water lapped against the sides of their boat with a pleasing sound. "What does the good book have to say about coincidence?"

Rex uttered a little laugh. "That doesn't exactly go along with omnipotence," he said. "In fact, it goes against the whole concept that God has everything in control, that it's all part of some supreme plan."

"So the Bible speaks against it?"

"Not explicitly, but the word is only in there one time. Christ speaks about it and it's a throwaway line, just something about the coincidence of a priest being somewhere at the right time. But he negates the idea in other places all through the New Testament. Think of the line about the sparrow."

"Which one is that?" Dave said, knowing that Rex sometimes forgot that not everyone was a walking concordance the way he was.

"He said not even a sparrow falls to the ground without our Father's notice, that God knows every hair on our heads, that everything is part of His master plan. So the Bible would be the place to go to look for proof against coincidence, not in favor of it."

"Well, on that count I agree with the Bible," Dave said. "I've been thinking about that boat Jesse brought in. He found it drifting right about here. He said the mouth of Catfish Cove. So I'm wondering if you'd have any idea what direction it might have come from."

"The current follows the old path of the rivers, and this would have been where the Big Laurel came through."

Dave had always been amazed by the way the lake current remembered where the rivers had flowed before. There was something almost mystical about that, the way people said there were holy places because of confluences or mountaintops.

"So the boat would have come from back our way," Rex continued, eyeing the lake. His face was lit with the golden glints of sunlight reflecting on the water. "Unless it got turned around in a storm, but usually the storms blow this way, too, south to north, same direction as the current through here."

"It's hard to know exactly, because of the storm that happened yesterday, then," Dave said.

"It's hard to know where exactly, period," Rex said. "But I can guarantee you it came from that way." He pointed back toward the marina and the fishing camp. "Had to. This current looks easy, but it's strong on a hollow thing like a boat."

"How long do you reckon it would take for a boat to drift to Catfish Cove from, say, the fishing camp?"

"That would depend on the time of day, the wind, lots of variables. Maybe the boat washed up on a bank and got caught there for a while. Maybe it just sailed straight on through open water. Could take a couple hours, could take a whole day."

"So the only thing we know for sure is it came from the south."

"If I was a betting man," Rex said, and nodded with certainty. "What are you thinking?"

"I'm thinking the killer used that boat to get to the fishing camp, then left in it, going back to wherever they had left their vehicle."

"Why not just drive into the fishing camp, park up the mountain a ways, and walk down there, then run back to their car and take off? Seems like being on a boat makes you more visible."

"But if you need to get from one point of the lake to another, it takes a lot less time by water than it does by car. Let's say the killer lived in Shady Grove. To get to the fishing camp by water would take twenty minutes if they parked their car on a road that crosses one of these ridges, then got into the boat and took off. But it'd take them an hour to drive all the way around the lake from Shady Grove to the fishing camp."

"Right. Of course. And if they're crossing the lake at night with no lights on the boat then they're likely to not be seen by anyone," Rex offered just as Shorty hopped up in his lap.

Dave nodded.

"So we need to think about where the boat launches are besides the fishing camp and the marina," Rex said, massaging one of Shorty's silky ears between two fingers. She was sniffing the clean air with her eyes closed in contentment.

"There are only three others on the whole lake. And only one to the south," Dave said. The next two words he said were joined in unison by Rex saying them, too: "the Flatwoods."

"But why not at least tie the boat up if they didn't take time to load it back up instead of trying to sink it?" Dave said, talking to himself more than asking Rex.

"They wanted to eliminate the chance of it leading back to them."

"So they ended up doing the very thing that would lead it back to them by trying to sink it and doing a shoddy job of it." Dave thought for a minute. "The only reason they'd try to sink it, and do a bad job of it, is if they were working in a time frame and had to hurry."

"But so what if they used the boat? That still doesn't tell you anything to help figure out who they are."

"Maybe not," Dave said, "but maybe so. We'll see."

Dave pulled the rope to start the Evinrude back up, and they parted the water back toward home.

The air was warm and golden on their faces as they idled into the marina. The sun was going down and had left the whole world in its honeyed light, making everything seem softer and prettier. The smell of grilled food and charcoal and early campfires drifted across the water to them. Some kids were still in the water, and as they chugged into their spot near the office, everyone on their houseboats waved to them or called out.

He sat Shorty out on the wooden walkway and tied up the boat. Rex climbed out, empty-handed since after the first catch they had both decided to throw back all dozen of the nice bluegills they had caught without discussing why. Sometimes the only reason for a fishing trip was to be out on the water on a nice, quiet evening and those felt just as good, if not better, than when one came home loaded down with fish.

"I've got a meatloaf in the icebox. Join me tonight?"

"Sounds perfect," Dave said. "In about an hour?"

"You want to invite the redhead?"

"Nina?" Dave hesitated. He couldn't avoid her. In fact, he would have to broach the subject of her family's land ownership soon, but that'd have to wait for now. "I guess so."

"See you then, lad," Rex said, and Shorty followed him as he walked away to his houseboat before Dave noticed and called her back. She came running and shifted from one foot to the other, ready to get back to her boat as she knew it was her suppertime, too. She gave one sharp bark to remind him of this.

"In a minute, Short Stuff." Dave climbed out and crossed the walkway to where he had tied the drifting johnboat Jesse had brought in. He sat on the middle bench and took his time studying everything before him. He imagined that before the boat was sunken it most likely contained paddles, life vests, a coil of rope, the normal contents of a rowboat. But there was nothing except mud and a scattering of rocks. He bent and studied the floor more closely. The wood there was well-seasoned and sturdy. This was a good, solid boat, not one you'd just let go without looking for it. He got down on his hands and knees to look more closely. Nothing.

Shorty snapped another high bark: *Come on, it's suppertime.* Dave ignored her, so she sat down and decided to bathe herself while she waited. Still, she latched an occasional miffed eye on Dave to let him know she wasn't waiting forever.

He moved slowly along each bench, studying them closely, carefully. Nothing out of the ordinary. He examined every inch of the boat to make sure. There was some dark discoloration on the wooden floor, but that could be anything. Still, it needed further examination. If he was ruling coincidence completely out of this case—and he had to if he was going to solve it—then this damaged boat showing up just after two murders meant something. He'd ask Victor for permission to get the luminol kit on it. Might as well check to see if there was any evidence of blood. Luminol was expensive, but they had no other physical evidence to go on besides two bodies—one that had been left under a steaming stream of water and another that had been submerged in the lake. Plus, Mayor Atlas Boone had told Dave to let him know if he needed anything, and some extra funding for this would help mightily.

"All right, fatty," Dave said as he jumped onto the dock. "Let's get you some supper." Shorty was so excited she ran ahead of him until he had to call her to slow down. She looked back at him impatiently until he caught up, even though she knew the way back to her boat just fine without him.

Chapter 24

Dave had an hour to kill before supper, so he put Eddy Arnold on his record player and sat with Shorty on his lap, looking out at the aching blue of the lake while he tapped his foot to "A Full Time Job." He hadn't been sitting long when he felt the jostling of Nina's houseboat next to his when she arrived home from work. He could hear her moving through the boat in the minutes before she slid open her door and came out onto her own porch to breathe in the lake after a long day at work.

"Well, hey there," she said, more to Shorty than Dave. Shorty's wagging tail was beating hard against Dave's chest.

"Long day?"

"Lord yes," Nina said. "I thought I was coming back to sleepy little Shady Grove after working at the Birmingham paper, and turns out there's more than plenty going on here. A wrecked chicken truck. A trash fire out of control up on Slate Ridge. Not to mention two murders."

"Never a dull moment," Dave said. "Do you have plans for supper?"

"I had planned on eating leftover chicken salad on saltines, like a real journalist would."

"Rex is making a meatloaf and requests our company. Seven thirty."

"You won't have to twist my arm," she said, stretching her arms over her head now and accompanying this with a yawn.

"I need to ask you a few questions, Nina. Formally."

She straightened up and furrowed her brow. "That sounds ominous."

"Just clearing some things up."

"Okay, let's hear it."

"Now?"

"Yep, let's get it over with."

"Did you know that Salem Campbell bought up your mother's family land at a rock-bottom price without telling them it would soon be waterfront property?"

She let out a sharp laugh. "Of course. Heard my mother complain about that my whole life. But she didn't hate him as much as my father did."

"Was his family property bought by Salem, too?"

"No, he just blamed Salem for having to move out of the valley. He felt like Salem should have pushed for the valley to be preserved instead of encouraging the TVA to come in and build the lake here," she said. "He knew the farmland was worth more than any economy brought in by the lake ever would be. He never got over the old confluence being flooded over, all the caves that were lost to the lake, all the history. I know the lake is beautiful, but I think he was right."

"I grieve over everything that was lost to the lake, too, but I can't help but think it improved our economy."

"That's mayor-talk," she said, not unkindly. "You had to say that so much when you were in office that you believe it. But when you look at the statistics it just doesn't pan out, Dave. The lake coming in took the people's independence, their ability to live off their own land. Made them dependent on tourists. And most of those tourists don't spend more than twenty dollars a trip when they come here. They buy some gas and food, but that's about it. Meanwhile, their traffic keeps our roads torn up and takes our tax dollars to repair them. They litter. Because when you're not from a place, you don't care as much about it. Lots of them treat locals like they're stupid hillbillies."

"Well, we could go back and forth about all that all night."

"Believe me, I've done the research," she said.

"Why?"

"Because I've been wanting to write about it for a while. I want to pitch to a big paper about it. The *Tennessean*, maybe. The *Louisville Times*. Maybe even the *New York Times*. There's a story there worth telling."

"So you know where that land is, that your family owned?"

"My mother always said it was where Salem built his mansion."

"That's right," Dave said. "Can you tell me where you were Thursday?"

A smile covered her face but she reconsidered and this turned to a scowl, causing lines to arise on her forehead. For a half second her cool disappeared, and he thought she might be nervous. Still, she hid it well. She sighed, smoothed her hair back, and eased out to the edge of her chair. "I worked all day. Went into the office at eight thirty that morning and didn't leave until around six thirty. Picked up supper at the Dixie and went straight back to my room."

"At the Town Square Hotel."

"That's right," she said.

"So lots of people would be able to back you up on that?"

"Everyone at the paper. Steve Berry at the Dixie. I'm sure Marjorie Thomas could. She's always at her little perch at the front desk at the hotel, nosey as can be." Nina stood, looked out at the lake, then back to Dave. "I know you're just doing your job, but how could you think that—"

"And then Saturday night, before you came out onto this porch and I saw you. What had your day entailed?"

"I left the hotel around nine and came straight here. Rex showed me the houseboat, and I gave him a deposit to hold it for me. I went back to the hotel and packed up my stuff and brought it all back here. By that time I guess it was around one thirty," she said. Now she was speaking to him in an overly formal way to emphasize how ridiculous she thought it was to be questioned.

"There's no use in being a smart aleck," Dave said, as kindly as he could. "You're a reporter. You've been on a crime beat. You know how this goes. I have to ask everyone involved."

"But I'm not involved."

"You know what was written on that shower house wall," Dave said, not adding that an iteration of it was also written on a note with Salem's clothes because she most likely didn't have that detail yet, and he wasn't about to let it slip. "So you know I'm looking at family histories in relation to the Campbell family. Your family had bad blood with him. So I have to talk to you."

"You don't have to accuse me of murder, though," she said, and crossed her arms as if cold, although the evening was still hot.

"I'm not. I'm checking all the boxes so I have a record of where everyone concerned was on the day of the murder," he said. "So let's get back to your timeline. That takes us up to the early afternoon. What next?"

"I drove to Nashville. Took me two hours. There's an artsy Katharine Hepburn film playing there. *Summertime.* I met a friend there, to see it, and I have my ticket stub in my purse. The movie lasted a couple hours, then we went to the Mercantile for a long supper—"

"I'll need that friend's name."

"Jake Fox. I'll get you his phone number. He works at the Nashville paper; used to be at the Birmingham paper. And before you get the wrong idea, he's not that kind of friend. I'm not his type."

"What's that supposed to mean?"

"He doesn't like girls, Dave. I know that probably shocks you."

He was only shocked that she'd speak so openly about it. Dave had had a pining for a friend of his in the army, but he wasn't about to mention that. He especially wasn't about to mention that one night he had found out Rob carried the same torch for him. And he certainly wasn't going to mention that he occasionally thought of Rob and what they had done several hot summer nights while stationed in Berlin, either. So no, he wasn't shocked, but he wasn't about to let her know either way. "Go on," he said, glancing at his watch. Rex hated for people to be late for meals.

"We finished around eight, I think, and we went to the Carousel Club in Printer's Alley."

"Who was playing?"

"A great piano player. Floyd something. Cramer, I think. Jake will know for sure. We left there around ten but I'd had one drink too many to drive home, so we went for a walk down by the river and I left Nashville around midnight. Drove straight back here—took me longer coming back because I'm a little night blind—and then I was with you."

"Did you see anything unusual when you were driving in, once you got close to the lake?" He was thinking about where the person in the boat might have made landfall before they tried to sink it. Maybe their car had been parked up on the marina road and they had run back through the woods to it.

She looked confused. "No," she said, but then second-guessed herself. Thought about it. "No. If I had, I would have mentioned it to you after the murder. Besides, why would I see something on the opposite side of the lake from the fishing camp?"

"Just checking," Dave said. "Anything else you can think to tell me that might be important?"

"Absolutely not," she said, unable to hide how insulted she was.

"Before coming back here to work for the paper, had you been in touch with anyone at all who lives in Shady Grove or around the lake?"

"No," she said. More quietly: "The only person I would've wanted to have been in contact with was you."

"There's something you're not telling me," he said, taking a chance that this bluntness might pump something out of her.

"About that night?"

"No, in general. For some reason I don't completely believe you."

"Well, that's your problem," she said, miffed now.

"All right then," he said, surprised by the note of finality in his own voice.

Nina had heard it, too, so she stood. "If we're done, *Deputy*, I think I'll change before supper."

"We're done," he said. Only when she had gone in did he realize the album had long ago reached its last song. The sounds of the lake were pleasant: the water against the side of the boats and the dock, the insects hollering from the trees along the bank, the frogs who popped their heads above water just enough to look around and call out. The moon eased out of the clouds and ran a jagged silver line on the water. Even though he was hungry and knew that supper would be waiting soon, he wished he could sit there the rest of the night and not move a muscle.

The more he thought about all of this, the more the puzzle pieces were going together in his mind. He still didn't know who had killed Esau and Salem, but he knew that he would before too much longer.

Chapter 25

The next morning Dave drove into town to meet with Noble, whom Sheila had arranged to be at the office by nine. Dave grabbed a cup of coffee from the percolator in the hallway and breezed into the interrogation room where Noble sat, looking mighty miffed to be there.

"I was aiming to mow my hay this morning," Noble said by way of greeting.

"Hopefully this won't take long, then," Dave said as he opened his notebook and clicked the silver button at the end of his pen, mostly to signal that he was ready to take notes. "I'll get right to it, Mr. Noble. I've learned that you dated Celeste Campbell as a young man."

Noble gave a little laugh. "I wouldn't hardly call it dating. We courted for a bit, but it didn't last long."

"She says it ended because you were too possessive."

Noble tensed at that. Then: "I could've had any girl I wanted back then," he said, paused, but then he couldn't seem to make himself stop talking. "Women are always saying things like that about men," he added.

"A woman's never said that about me, sir," Dave said. He was glad to see this was getting a rise out of the man.

"Maybe not to your face," Noble said, but he wasn't about to belabor the point. "Listen, that was decades ago. I dated a lot of girls. I barely remember her. But I've never been possessive over anybody."

Dave did not believe that for a second. "If you barely remember her, I wonder why you were following her a couple of weeks ago." Dave watched as that landed on Noble's ears. He was a cool character, though, because he didn't react right away.

After a moment Noble shifted in his chair as if he might rise and leave the room but instead he threw his shoulders back and rolled his head around his neck, issuing a loud pop. Dave thought the man was buying himself time to construct a lie but then he said, "I did follow her. She's telling the truth about that."

"Why would you do that?"

"I hadn't thought of her, for years. But then I was at a four-way intersection and there she was. I recognized her, even though I hadn't seen her in all those years. She's a striking woman. And I don't know. It was foolish of me. I'm embarrassed to admit it."

"Let's hear it," Dave said.

"I've been back here about six months. Moved back when my daddy died."

"Yes, you told me that."

"And well, I've just been so lonesome. I haven't seen hardly anybody since I got back. All my family is dead. I was gone from here for decades. Lost touch with folks. And it's just been me, out there at my parents' place. When I saw her, for some reason, I thought if I followed her she might pull into a store in town and I'd pull in beside her, act like I had just happened upon her and we'd chat for a bit. I just wanted some company." Noble was looking Dave directly in the eye. "But she didn't stop. She kept driving, and for some reason I kept following her until we got out near the Nashville Pike. She pulled to the shoulder of the road, but we were out there in the country and it would've seemed strange for me to pull up behind her there. It might have scared her. So I just drove on past, and I didn't think much of it."

All of that checked out exactly as Celeste had told Dave. "Did you know she was married to Salem Campbell?"

"Not until I read it in the newspaper yesterday."

"And did you know Salem?"

"No. I've been gone all these years. But like anybody else who's ever lived here, I know who he is. Was."

Noble seemed just embarrassed and forthcoming enough to be believable, but Dave didn't want to let him know that. He pulled a suspicious face and closed his notebook.

"All right then, Mr. Noble. That's all I have. For *now*." He put an emphasis on the "now" just to keep the man dangling on a hook. "I'll let you get to that hay."

"Yeah, now that I've lost the cool part of the day," Noble said. He was a man who liked to get the final word.

Chapter 26

For the past couple of hours, Dave and Victor had been going over everything they knew thus far:

The connections between Nina, Steve Berry, and Salem Campbell. The strange distrust he had for Nina despite also feeling bound to her across time since their childhoods. The fact that he knew for sure Steve Berry was an adulterer. That didn't mean he was a killer of course, but it did mean he was a good liar.

The drifting boat.

The fact that Noble had known Esau's stepmother and Salem's wife in the far past. He needed to look into what Noble had been doing in his years away from the lake. Talk to folks who knew him. Talk to him again, too. Shoot, he did not want to go back out to Fogtown, where Noble was living now. He didn't ever want to go back there.

The suspicion that hung over Ron Rose all these years after the murder of his mother; Denise Rose's willingness to clobber someone who insulted her. The Roses were still at their fishing tournament and nothing seemed amiss with them, but of course they'd be smart to lay low if they had done anything here, wouldn't they? The only personal connection at all there was that Esau had insulted Denise.

Then there was Frank White, a man who reeked of desperation whether it was about gambling debts or his dying child. And a desperate man was capable of anything.

The only person at the camp who seemed a void was Tom. Maybe Dave had missed something there, but he had just seemed like a lonesome old farmer who came to the lake to think about old times when he and his wife had taken their child to the confluence of the rivers. He, like everyone else on this case, had lost something because of the creation of the lake, and it seemed like most everyone blamed Salem Campbell for that. Salem had been the living embodiment of the loss they all shared.

Another connection was Celeste Campbell, who had not been unfriendly to him but in looking back over their interview, he realized he would need to speak to her again because really she had answered exactly what he asked and nothing more. That was the sign of someone who had something to hide.

Dave had just filled Victor in on Celeste Campbell's responses, and they discussed the fact that they couldn't hold Frank White much longer despite his attempt to flee the interrogation. As they were talking about him, Sheila opened the door only wide enough to stick her head in.

"Sheriff, we need you," she said, out of breath from running down the hallway. "Right now."

As they hustled down the corridor that connected the sheriff's office to the jail, Sheila explained that Frank was the issue.

"His wife is raising hell about him being held," she said. "Zeke got smart with her, but she's not the kind of woman that works on."

When they reached the jail reception area, Loretta White was pacing back and forth like an enraged animal in a pen. She was a hard-faced woman with high cheekbones, a sharp nose, and a wild mane of black hair she had pinned up in the front to keep out of her tired eyes. She was one of those country women who had known hard work her whole life and had never been stymied by it; in fact, she was probably a lot like Dave's aunts, who had delighted in being built for hard work. As soon as she saw the badge on Victor's chest, she flew toward him.

"My child is dying and I had to leave her for the first time in months to come here. I want my husband released, *right* now."

"If you can talk to us a few minutes and clear some things up—"

"Ask me anything," she said, more angry than helpful. "I don't have anything to hide. I left my sick little girl with my mother and drove two hours to get here, and I am taking Frank home with me."

Victor led her back to the interrogation room and sent Sheila for coffee for all three of them. He gave Dave a silent look that let him know he should do the questioning. But he didn't have to ask a thing before she spilled all they needed to know.

"Frank is a good man, but he hasn't dealt with our daughter's illness in a good way. It's made him do stupid things," she said. Dave noticed that her hands were raw and red. "Frank couldn't take seeing her suffer. He's not strong. Not in that way." She squared her shoulders. "Women usually are. Stronger, that way. You know. So I haven't left her side, but occasionally Frank just has to leave or he'll have a breakdown. This has been going on for two years, our daughter. Last year he came down to the fishing camp, just to settle his mind for a day. But that night he played cards with Esau Campbell. And the game got so big that Esau ended up betting the fishing camp. Frank won it."

A thrill ran through Dave. Frank had won the *entire* fishing camp? This was great information, and especially important was that Frank had withheld such a detail.

"But this Esau wouldn't turn over the deed. Frank had won it, fair and square. But what else could he do? Wasn't like the police were going to force Campbell to give him the camp. It was just the two of them gambling. Finally, Esau told him he didn't even own the camp; it belonged to his father."

The more she talked, the worse all of this looked for Frank, Dave thought. Apparently his instinct had been wrong about the man. The woman had taken a breath and paused long enough that Dave started to ask her what happened next but before he could, she started talking again.

"So he came home. And really, he didn't want the man's property. But the principle of it ate at him, being cheated that way. Then the hospital bills really piled up and Frank called and told Esau that he'd forget about the camp deed if he'd just give him five hundred dollars and be done with it. We needed that money for the treatments."

She stopped, looking at first Dave and then Victor as if this settled everything.

"But we know that your husband gambled with Mr. Campbell again, Mrs. White," Dave said, as gently as he could. This was all leading somewhere; he could feel it. "Both nights before Mr. Campbell was killed. So why would he do that if he had already been cheated by him?"

"Campbell gave him the five hundred dollars, the night he arrived," she said, and then tears sprang into her eyes. Dave saw they were the results of anger, years of frustration with her husband. "But Frank is *so* damn stupid, he got pulled in again. I love him, and in many ways he can be so smart, but sometimes he's *so stupid*." She paused long enough to gather herself and plowed on. "Frank saw that Esau had more money and he thought he'd get more of it. And he did, the first night. But then the second night, he lost it all again."

"But the stakes at the game that night weren't that high," Dave said. "The other men there said the winnings were no more than a hundred dollars."

"Frank didn't gamble the five hundred. He put that aside."

So Frank had been telling the truth about everything.

"How do you know this?" Dave asked.

"He called me, Saturday morning. He told me all of that. He was talking so fast I had to make him slow down. And he told me that Esau had been found dead. He had gone to the payphone at the top of the hill to report it to the police, so he called me, too."

"Did it cross your mind that he killed Mr. Campbell?"

She looked befuddled at the question. "Of course not," she said. "I'm telling you, Frank can be so dumb I feel like shaking him, but he's good to the bone. He's always had a gambling problem, but I've mostly kept it in check ever since we've been married. But he won't even kill a spider. He scoops them up in a towel and throws them out the door."

"And what did you say, when he told you all of this that morning?"

"I told him to come home, right then. He said he had to be questioned. Abra had taken a turn for the worse and I thought she was leaving us. I was afraid she'd not make it through the day, so I was screaming for him to just come home, and I hung up on him."

"If he still had the five hundred dollars, why did he ransack the house?"

"He wouldn't do that," she said, her eyes firmly set on Dave's. *This woman was too good for Frank White*, he thought. "I know he wouldn't."

Dave thought maybe she was right.

"I just want him to come home to our daughter," she said, and now the anger that had built up in her became a deep sadness. Dave thought he had never seen anyone sadder in his life, and no wonder. He couldn't imagine what this family had been through. "Please, let him come home. I've never begged to anyone in my life, but if that's what it takes—"

Victor nudged his elbow gently against Dave's, so gently she wouldn't have even noticed.

"Give us just a minute, Mrs. White," Dave said, rising in unison with Victor. "We'll be back soon."

In the hallway, Victor leaned in so close Dave could smell the coffee on his breath. "What are you thinking?"

"I'm thinking we need to let him go home," Dave said. "Right now. He didn't do it."

"So who did?" Victor asked, and reached out to grab Dave's arm as he hurried away. He wasn't quick enough, though.

"I'm going to find out," Dave said, and headed back down the corridor to find Sheila so they could check out the research he had asked her to do that morning.

Chapter 27

Dave and Sheila worked the rest of the day, poring over every document they could find. Sheila had not only pulled items from county records but also from the local high schools and the public library. They broke only long enough for Dave to go fetch chili buns and fries from the Dixie Café, then they ate while they did their research. Naturally Sheila dropped mustard and chili onto some of the documents, but wiped them away with a dampened thumb and without a word.

They made connection after connection, mapping it all out on the green chalkboard behind them. Dave stood back from the board and considered it. All of the lines crisscrossing one another looked like a spider's web, but still, he knew that some strands were missing. They only had to figure out what.

Just as the bells on the Methodist church down the street chimed five o'clock, there was a tap on the door.

Collins leaned in and held out a manila envelope. "Luminol test on the boat is back," he said, as if bored.

Dave snatched the folder from him and sat down at the table, Sheila right at his shoulder.

He flipped through several pages of chemical percentages, explanations of how the luminol test worked, words like "chemiluminescence" and "intermolecular," illustrations of the boat's exterior from both sides and from above. Then, on the last page:

Blood is detected in the middle panel of the metal boat (see illustration) and is consistent with a large wound. Patterns detected show evidence of circular motions in the blood which suggest clean-up.

"By God, I knew it!" Dave said.

"Salem Campbell was killed in the boat," Sheila said.

"If we can find the trailer that brought the boat to the lake, that'll get us closer to who brought it. You know where we should start?"

Sheila was already on the phone, talking to Victor. "We need to get a team out to the fishing camp to search for the boat trailer. Dave thinks they may have let it roll into the lake, so out in the water from the boat ramp would be the first place to look."

"You're always one step ahead," he said when Sheila sat the phone on its cradle.

"Pays to be in this life," she said, and started clearing a space on the large table that was covered with books and documents. "So let's look back at whose paths have crossed with the Campbell family and put that together with who could have been in that boat with Salem," Sheila said. "And we need to start building timelines."

"Timeline, motive, opportunity," Dave said.

Every line of inquiry about Tom Jenkins kept going back to him leading a quiet life down in Cookeville. Hard worker, beloved by neighbors, no record. Seemed there was nothing to indicate any reason he might be involved. Still, Dave wasn't putting him completely off the table. If there was one thing Dave knew for certain, it was that still waters run deep.

Before they knew it, the church bells were calling out midnight.

★ ★ ★

Mist was still hovering like wintery breath just above the lake's surface as Dave pulled into the fish camp early the next morning. On the drive over, he had watched the sunrise stretching its rosy self out over the shoulders of the mountains. The dive team had driven in from Frankfort while it was still dark because they wanted to get in the water while it was as still as possible, with no boats churning up the undercurrent. Even if they had closed off this whole section of the lake, nothing would be as good as getting under the surface before anything but the fishes were moving. He could have driven a johnboat over here from the marina in about ten minutes, but he'd had to take the long drive around the lake to keep the waters still.

By the time he reached the water's edge, the two divers were going under right where he had told Victor they should check out: the area in front of the old boat ramp he had noticed on the large picture in Esau's cottage. This would have been the easiest place to get rid of a car or a boat trailer from the fish camp. The current boat ramp would have been too easy to figure out. Dave was betting that the killer had noticed the old boat ramp while they were in Esau's cabin, too. A man Dave didn't know sat in a wrecker, sloppily eating a honey bun while he waited in case the divers found anything he might attach to and pull out of the water.

Victor stood alone on the bank, watching. His uniform was neatly pressed and Dave imagined his old friend setting up the ironing board—cringing at its creakiness as it unfolded—and pressing his clothes while the night was still blue outside, moving quietly to avoid waking up Janet. She had always hated ironing above all other household chores, and as military men both Dave and Victor found order in it. He tamped down the tenderness he felt for Victor at this image and reminded himself of the movie in his head he had played over and over: the thought of Victor in bed with Janet. Or Victor easing apart the meeting of two curtains to peer out to make sure Dave was nowhere about as they had snuck around. His anger burned again. Yet not anger so much as a deep hurt, although he didn't like to admit that to himself. All of this would be much easier if he could hate Victor.

Dave planted himself ten yards down the lakeshore from Victor, close enough to have the same view of the divers but far enough away to let Victor know he didn't want to be near him. Victor strolled over to him anyway.

"Morning, Dave," Victor said when he drew near.

Dave's only response was to tighten the muscle in his jaw. He kept his eyes on the surface of the water, which was as still and flat as a sheet of glass, even with the divers moving about beneath it.

"Not even going to exchange a greeting with me now?" Victor asked.

"I'll talk to you about this murder investigation," Dave said. "That's it."

"I don't know what to do, Dave. I know that apologizing ain't enough. I know that trying to make up for it ain't even enough. There's no way to make up for it. I know that what I did is unforgiveable." Victor paused as if to give Dave the chance to reply but Dave only studied the water, not seeing so much as a bubble out there. "But I'll do whatever it takes to at least not have you hate me. I can understand why you do, but I'll do whatever you want. I'll even beg to you."

Dave let a silence stand between them for a full couple of minutes, and then he said, quietly: "There's nothing you can do, Victor. You destroyed our friendship and that's all there is to it. It's the same difference as killing somebody: once it's done, there's no undoing it. So quit dreaming that might happen. It won't."

"I'm not happy," Victor said, "if it's any consolation."

Dave wasn't sure if he would have responded to that or not, and he didn't have to because just then one of the divers popped to the surface and thrust a thumbs-up into the air.

Dave remained where he was while Victor consulted with the wrecker driver, who backed his vehicle down the old boat ramp. The man stopped with his rear wheels out in the water so the chain on the back of the truck would reach far out into the water. He dropped it enough for one of the divers to catch hold and they disappeared again. The wrecker driver flipped a large metal switch on the side of the truck and the winch began winding in the chain, making a mighty racket on the morning calm as it pulled in the boat trailer. Once they repeated the process they found an even bigger catch: Salem Campbell's gold-colored Cadillac.

Chapter 28

"I knew you'd be back," the housekeeper, Carol Ann, said when she opened the door a couple hours later. Dave had already had an eventful morning out at the fishing camp, but now he needed more answers.

He was surprised by this greeting, but even more when she stepped back so he could enter and he saw the suitcases in the foyer.

"Mrs. Campbell is going somewhere?"

Carol Ann nodded. "Nashville. Back and forth, back and forth, all the time," she said.

"She told me she always left very early," Dave said, and glanced down at his watch. "It's a quarter to ten."

"She's waiting for Patricia—her daughter—to arrive."

The click of Celeste's heels on the tiled hallway announced her before she came around the corner, pulling on a pair of short gloves with a smile on her face that dropped away as soon as she saw Dave. "I thought surely it was Patricia," she said.

"I'm sorry to disappoint you, Mrs. Campbell."

Her smile seemed forced even though she was putting on her best effort. "How can I help you?"

"I just needed to ask you a few more questions. I'm sorry to bother you again."

Celeste turned toward the sitting room to Dave's right, the one with the black-lacquered piano. "We can sit in here." When he stepped in she was standing by her chair, so he stood at the one across from her, not about to sit first. "Do you want coffee or tea, Deputy? A Co-cola?"

"No, no, I just had—"

"Go on then, Carol Ann," she said, and the housekeeper seemed to snap out of some reverie that had befallen her while she stood in the wide doorway to the room. For a second Dave thought the woman might defy Celeste and not leave, but then she did.

Celeste sat down and spread the sides of her skirt out, tugging the hem down to cover her knees. "Is there new information?"

He decided to throw her off-kilter by not answering her. "May I ask where you're headed?"

"I'm going back to Nashville. It's too lonesome here. Too quiet. I want to be back in the city."

"But what about the funerals?"

"The sheriff said it'd be at least a week before Salem's body is released. I might as well spend that time in the city where I have a support system. People here don't like me much, Deputy. As you probably know."

"No, I don't know that. I think people here feel they don't know you."

"I left as soon as I graduated high school and went to Nashville. I swore I'd never come back here. But when I met Salem . . . Well, it all made sense, and I thought living like this"—she raised her hand and swept it through the air, indicating the wealth around them—"would make me happy. I don't guess that's in the cards for me."

"But you said you and Esau were close. His body will be released tomorrow."

She brushed some unseen lint off her skirt with the side of her hand, not meeting Dave's eyes. "I've arranged everything for Esau. The funeral home will take care of him. I'd be the only person there, and that's too embarrassing. Esau will never know the difference. But I made sure he had only the best of everything. Does that seem cruel to you?"

Maybe not cruel, he thought, *but cold*. "That's not for me to judge," he said. "Why didn't you mention that your father and Salem had trouble in the past?"

"My father died long before I ever married Salem."

"This was before you ever met Salem. You had already left home when Salem bought bottomland from your father a few months before the Corps of Engineers would have offered him twice the amount for the building of the lake. Forgive me, ma'am, but it's hard to believe that your parents didn't mention it at the time or that Salem didn't mention it later."

"My father was always angry at somebody, Deputy. Did he file a complaint about it or something?"

Not that Dave or Sheila had found. But they had found where Salem had bought up a huge parcel of the Saylor land three months before the Corps started to put in their offers.

He was assuming that Celeste's father was just as upset about it as Nina and Steve Berry had told him their fathers had been. But he wasn't here to answer her questions, so he went on his own track.

"You also didn't tell me you had loaned Esau money." Another guess, but as soon as he said it, he saw her face change enough to know he was right. Where else would Esau have gotten the money to pay off Frank White?

"I didn't think that mattered. I told you that I went to see him."

"Why not tell me that, then?"

"I don't know why, to be honest," she said. She tugged a handkerchief from the left sleeve of her dress even though there were no tears in her eyes. She folded it into a small, neat rectangle as she talked. "I was upset. My husband and my stepson had just been found murdered. I wasn't exactly thinking straight."

"I think you were fed up with Esau getting into scrapes. You told me you and Esau were close, but I haven't found any proof of that," Dave said, trying to antagonize her enough to see what passions lay beneath that cool exterior. "Nobody who knew either of you has backed that up. In fact, when one of our deputies talked to your daughter at the university, she told him Esau had always been a thorn in your side."

"You can't be questioning my daughter!" Her voice was high, sharp. He was surprised the young woman hadn't told her; she had probably known how her mother would react and had hoped to save the sheriff's department from experiencing her wrath.

"Of course I can, ma'am. She's nineteen years old. An adult."

Celeste took a deep breath, but her anger showed red in her flushed cheeks. She bent forward and removed the lid from a marble box full of rolled cigarettes. Her hands were steady when she picked up the slender silver lighter beside the box and held the flame before her face. Now she breathed out a firm line of smoke and seemed to have regained her bearing.

"Do you want to tell me about that?"

"I don't see why I should tell you anything. I'm not under arrest, and you're being accusatory in a way that I find offensive."

"I'm just trying to check all the boxes, Mrs. Campbell," he said. "But what I can't figure out is why you took him the five hundred dollars if you didn't get along with him. It doesn't make much sense."

She took a hard drag on the cigarette, watching him over the burning tip. He decided he wouldn't speak again until she did. He'd let the silence work on her.

"My daughter wouldn't know, Deputy. Like I told you before, Salem always made sure she wasn't around Esau. When I spoke to him, it was always in secret. I felt sorry for him—his mother had died when he was a boy and I was the only mother figure he had in his life. I know what that's like. My mother died when I was young. And even though he wasn't the kind of person I—or anybody—could get close to, there was something in me that was protective of him. Still, that doesn't mean I ever wanted him around Patricia."

"Okay," Dave said, and wrote down *Okay, keep her talking don't stop now* on his notepad; she couldn't see what he was writing, but the fact that he was taking notes seemed to urge her to keep going.

"Esau and I weren't best friends, but we were often united in keeping his father's temper at bay. He told me he had run into some real trouble and needed a thousand dollars."

Dave wrote this down: *$1000*. Frank had asked for five hundred dollars, so where had the rest of it gone? Assuming she was being honest. Esau had likely felt that if he was borrowing money he might as well get a bit extra for himself, too. Still, Dave hadn't found one penny at Esau's cottage, so that extra five hundred had gone somewhere.

She went on. "I don't usually carry that kind of money with me, but I was on my way to Nashville that morning when I dropped in on him, and I had taken some out of the safe. I was feeling blue, and planned to have a little splurge. And I wasn't just dropping in out of the kindness of my heart. To tell you the truth, I wanted to peek in on him to see how well he was keeping everything going there."

"And?"

"I was impressed," she said. "I told you this before. Everything looked in order. The camp was clean, well-kept. The customers looked happy."

"So you dropped the money off and you left for Nashville, and the next thing you know, your stepson and your husband are dead."

"That's right. I told Esau that I'd never give him any more money and that if he ever asked me again, I'd just let

Salem deal with him. In the past he always thought he could woo me back to his side, but this time I could tell, he knew I meant business."

"You said the customers seemed happy. Did you meet any of them?"

"No. I saw a couple drinking coffee on their porch, laughing with each other. A woman who looked like Marilyn Monroe and a little round man. And down on the dock I could see another man, casting out lines. Another one working on something. Cleaning fish, maybe? Everything seemed pleasant and in order."

"But you never spoke to any of them?"

"No. Only Esau."

"And the men on the dock. Can you describe them?"

She thought about this for a moment, then shook her head. "No, the sun was behind them, so I couldn't see anything. The one fishing was tall, slender." She paused to think, narrowing her eyes as if she could see the image of the memory on the wall in front of her and was squinting to see better. "The other one shorter, a little paunch. Maybe older. That's all I know."

Then Dave came to the main reason he was there today. When he told her where they had found Salem's car, she immediately knew what this meant.

"So someone at that fishing camp killed him."

"Or at least someone familiar enough with it to know an unused boat ramp still existed, out of the way."

"Then took his body to the Flatwoods," she said. "But why?" She had put her hand over her mouth and now spoke through the gaps between her fingers.

Dave shrugged. "We'll figure that out soon enough." He turned to a page in his notebook where he had written down the names of all the people present at the fishing camp before he came to Celeste's house. He read over the names again:

Tom Jenkins
Burgess Noble
Ron and Denise Rose
Frank White

When he ripped the page from his notebook, Celeste jumped as if startled. He had thought he might have her read the list again, just as he had the first time he'd been here, to see which names were familiar, but then he reconsidered, decided to read them out loud. But first, he wanted to know more about Noble.

"What more can you tell me about Burgess Noble?"

"I told you, I hadn't thought about him in years until I thought I recognized him on the road that day—"

"Tell me about when you did know him."

Celeste's hands were shaking. He saw her adjusting and readjusting a ruby ring that sat in an intricate setting above her silver wedding band.

"We went to high school together, but he was three years older than me." Dave already knew this; in her research on Celeste Campbell, Sheila had rounded up every yearbook from each year Celeste had attended high school in Bonnytown. Sharp-eyed as always, she had found Burgess Noble's picture a couple pages away from Celeste's—he was a senior when she was a sophomore, so their paths there had only crossed briefly. This is why Dave was here.

To rule out another coincidence. And they needed to know more about how well these two had known each other.

"And as I said, we dated, briefly."

"How briefly?"

"I told you already, about six months, I guess. Brief, but intense—" Celeste paused, took another cigarette from the box and lit it off the embers of her last one. "I had a terrible crush on him at the time. He was handsome. But I was just a girl and he was already a man, even as a senior in high school."

"What happened?"

"He was too jealous, too controlling. Most men are. Even as boys. But." He saw that she was recalling something disturbing. She was no longer looking at him, but at the floor, her brow furrowed. "Well, Deputy, I've put most of this out of my mind."

"Anything you remember may help us figure out who killed your husband and stepson, Mrs. Campbell."

She put her eyes back on his. "One day we were sitting on my porch, alone. My father was down in the fields. Burgess was complaining because I had spoken to a boy at school. A friend I'd known my whole life. He grabbed hold of my wrist, hard. It hurt. When he saw I was scared of him, he started begging me to forgive him. But I told him it was over, that I wasn't putting up with that. He raised his hand to slap me, but I dodged him, and he missed. But he was going to. There was some stove wood stacked up on the porch and I grabbed one of the logs, told him he better get the hell away from me."

"And he did?"

"Yes, he left."

"You'd never seen him get violent before then?"

"No. Later I realized that he was too serious about me from the start. Too . . . worshipful. But never anything violent. As soon as it happened I told my father and he found him, told him to leave me alone. Whatever Daddy said to him worked because I never heard from him again. He avoided me at school and as soon as he graduated, he left the area. Someone told me he ended up working on a fishing boat or a steamboat on the Mississippi River. That's it."

"And you knew your housekeeper growing up, is that right?"

"Yes. Carol Ann. We lost touch after high school, but before that we were close—"

"I'd like to speak to her."

Immediately Celeste called the woman's name and she appeared too quickly, revealing that she had been hovering in the foyer the entire time. She seemed to only realize how obvious this was once she had made herself known. She folded her hands in front of herself and didn't say anything, looking at both of them with expectation.

"Do you remember Burgess Noble?"

"Yes, but I never really knew him. I mostly remember him because Celeste courted him a little while. But that was so long ago."

Dave looked down at the list, angry at himself for not having interviewed her more closely when he had first been here. It was a stupid mistake on his part to ignore someone because they were the help. He was from the kind of raising that should have known better than that, and now he felt badly for overlooking this woman the way he had. "Have you ever heard of Ron or Sheila Rose?"

She shook her head, no.

"Tom Jenkins?"

She looked confused. "I was married to Tom straight out of high school."

That was certainly not a connection he had been expecting but he didn't show her that, hopeful she might think he already knew this.

"Did he know Burgess Noble back then, too?"

Carol Ann seemed to not quite wrap her mind around this question for a moment, but then she replied, "No, Tom's not from here. Lived a couple hours off, down in Cookeville. I met him when my brother moved down there and I went to visit. They worked together at the mill."

"When we first met, you said you 'lost' your first husband. I thought that meant he had passed away."

The housekeeper looked down at her liver-spotted hands. "Being divorced is not something I generally like to announce to people."

"I'm sorry to ask you about a delicate matter, Miss Gabbard, but—"

"Mrs. Gabbard," she said. "I remarried a long time ago, and my husband passed a few years back."

"What happened to your and Tom Jenkins's marriage?"

"He left me for another woman, Deputy. It's all in the past and—"

"And would you think of Tom Jenkins as a violent man?"

"No," she said, instantly. She was pretty even as an older woman and in that moment Dave could picture how lovely she must have been as a young bride. "I always thought he was the best thing that ever happened to me, but you can never completely know somebody, can you? We had a beautiful boy together and I thought we had a good life, but one day he came in and told me he was in love with somebody else. That's that."

"And he had no connection at all to Salem Campbell or the lake that you knew of?"

"No, he didn't even know this area until he met me, and we only came up to visit my family occasionally."

"He mentioned to me that the two of you used to stop at the confluence of the three rivers and have picnics."

She thought for a second. "I guess we did. That was a whole other life, seems like. I was bitter over it all for years. It was shameful, in my family, to be divorced. But eventually people forgot, and I quit worrying so much about it. If it wasn't for having a son with him, I'd probably never even think of him."

"Was he a good father to your boy?"

"Well, he wasn't mean to him or anything, but he just never was there for him. The same way his own father did him."

Sins of the father, Dave thought.

"Anything else at all you remember about Burgess Noble or Tom Jenkins that might be helpful to me?"

The housekeeper had something on her mind; he could tell. But she was hesitating. Just when he was about to ask her to spit it out, she did.

"I don't know if it matters or not, but for a little while Burgess's stepdaddy pastored the church my parents went to. He didn't last there long; his preaching was too over-the-top for that congregation. And my mother. She always said he wasn't right."

"How do you mean?"

"Well, I remember her saying that he was mean to his wife, and to Burgess. He was real bad to"—she was struggling to say this part, but she did—"to beat them. Folks figured that's why Burgess went so far away as quick as he could."

Sins of the father.

"You said he was Noble's stepfather?"

"Yes, Waylon Boggs." Dave knew that name, but he didn't know how. He knew that he had heard it before, just recently, but there was too much information racing around in his mind for him to light on that information right now. And the woman had suddenly turned into a chatterbox. She went on: "I don't know why I remember his name. I guess because it was unusual, and different from Burgess's. I believe his real daddy died when he was very young."

"And Burgess's mother died of cancer when we were in high school," Celeste said. "I remember that. So it would have just been Burgess and this stepfather at home."

Down the hall Dave heard a grandfather clock chime out ten deep tones. A thought suddenly struck him. "Mrs. Campbell, how late is your daughter?"

"She should have been here a couple hours ago. She's never late, and she knows I like to get on the road early. I'm starting to get a little worried—"

"Was she traveling alone?"

"Yes," Celeste said. "I wanted to send a driver up there to get her, but she's a wild spirit. Her biggest issue her whole life is seeing herself and her own family as *bourgeoisie*. That's her favorite insult—"

Dave jumped to his feet. "Ma'am, I need you to stay here until you hear from me. All right?" She nodded. "Deputy Collins will be here to guard your place until further notice. Do not leave the house."

Just as he went out the door, he remembered exactly where he had heard the name Waylon Boggs.

Chapter 29

Fogtown was about as far back in the hills as a person could get nowadays, and Burgess Noble lived as far back as a person could go. The deepest valleys were under the lake now, and the biggest mountains now supped at the water's edge. But Fogtown was far up the stretch of the Big Laurel River that hadn't been flooded for the lake and remained the most remote section of the whole region. A deceptive name as there was no town here at all. A holdover from when there had been a big Shawnee settlement here as late as the 1700s. No trace of that now, though, except a few of the Shawnee grave mounds that had survived. Electric lines had not been run into the area yet because there weren't enough families living up there to justify such an extravagance.

The roads were not even graveled and today as they drove there, dust swirled behind them and resettled on the dusty trees lining the way. Victor was pushing the car as fast as he could handle it. Before leaving the office he had issued an APB for Noble so every cop in the area was on the lookout for him, but Dave and Victor were betting on him being at home. The mid-June day was sweltering, but the farther they went the thicker the dust became, so they had to roll up the windows on the police cruiser and take the heat to keep from breathing the dirt. The car was only ten years old but had been bought before air conditioning was readily available, so Victor had to bear the heat until the car either gave out or the budget was increased.

On either side of them the mountains rose steep and shadowy, tangles of huge laurel thickets and boulders and trees thick as ancient columns. Running parallel to the road at every turn was the Big Laurel River, not so deep here at its headwaters as it was nearer to the lake. In places it seemed no more than a wide, shallow creek, punctuated by gray rocks that had rolled out of the mountains and into its bed. There was beauty here but there was something else, too. Folks in these parts didn't say it aloud too often, but occasionally they did, and everyone knew it: there was something rotten about this place.

Dave believed in evil. He had seen it. At murder scenes. On battlefields. In a concentration camp. In his own father's eyes at his worst. While he would not have said this to anyone, he knew it at his core: an old, dark evil lurked in Fogtown. He felt it, crawling all over him like insects. During the Revolutionary War, a lost band of soldiers had massacred the Shawnee at Fogtown. Legend had it they committed atrocities there as well—atrocities so terrible that the land remembered them.

Dave had not been back to Fogtown since he was a rookie sheriff straight out of the army. He had been thrust into the most sensational murder case these parts had ever known, a case he tried to not think about although he still dreamed of those children sometimes.

Dave also had not been in a vehicle alone with Victor in a long while. More than two years, he thought. When they had been on the blacktopped and graveled roads, they had at least had their windows down and the rustling wind between them to distract from the silence between them. Now that the windows were up, Victor felt the need to break it.

"Problem is, all we have is a theory," Victor said. "No evidence at all."

"I'm betting that talking more to him will lead us to that. Or in the opposite direction. Either way, he's more of a puzzle piece in this than he first appeared."

"I don't know, Dave. I'm afraid we're walking on thin ice. We don't have a warrant or a—"

"Then why did you insist on coming with me?" Dave sounded more hateful than he felt, but he didn't care.

"Because you may be walking into harm's way."

"We don't need a warrant to ask the man a few more questions," Dave said. "And I'm hoping like hell that Patricia Campbell is just running late and that we won't find her up here with him."

"Well, if we do," Victor said, "then we sure won't need a warrant."

They rode along in silence for a moment. As they did a light rain began to fall, immediately wetting the dirt road enough for the dust to settle. The heat had built up so much that sweat was rolling down Dave's back. He and Victor both rolled their windows down enough for the air to come in.

"The thing is, the more I've thought about it, the more it's too big a coincidence," Dave said, speaking up over the wind whistling into the cab of the car. "For him to have known Salem's wife all those years ago and be at the exact spot where Salem's son is killed. To be on the same lake where Salem and his son are killed just a few days before. And I don't believe in coincidences."

The rain was little more than a thin mist, most likely the remnants of a thunderstorm that was wreaking its momentary drama over the big waters of Cedar Lake. Still, the world was cooling around them and already this place's namesake fog was rising up from the clefts between the mountains, from the rocky places that were the among the last truly wild places in this country.

"The drifting boat surely fits into this scenario just right. See, I had it backward at the beginning. I thought the boat had been used by the killer to get to the fishing camp to kill Esau. But the boat was used to get from the fishing camp to the Flatwoods, where the body was left. And we know the murder happened in the boat, yet Salem's clothes were stacked up on the bank at the Flatwoods. Again, to make it look like the murder happened there."

"So he made him strip down in the boat?"

"Or back at the fishing camp," Dave said.

"Doesn't make much sense, that part."

"Because he knew in advance where he was going and wanted to leave the clothes on the bank to make it look like he had come in by car, not boat." Dave had thought all this over a dozen times, and this was the only way that made total sense. "If it was Noble, or anybody else at the fishing camp, they would have wanted to draw attention away from the camp when it came to Salem. Esau was the only person at the camp when Noble arrived, so he'd be the only person who would have known if he brought a boat."

"Unless someone saw him on his way," Victor said.

"If we put that question out there, we might find someone who did," Dave said. "The thing is, he could have left the camp in the night without anyone knowing the difference."

"Still doesn't add up. How would he have gotten Salem down to the lake? You seriously think he just pulled up on the bank below Salem's mansion and Salem jumped in with him to be carried off to his death at the Flatwoods?"

"No, I think Salem was the other person who visited the camp that day," Dave told him. "Noble got him then."

"And hid his car by driving it down that old ramp into the lake," Victor said. "Still, we don't know if Noble did that or not."

"We will when we question him again. He answers our questions, lets us search for Patricia, and if all is clear then we'll move onto the next theory. He'll either rule himself out. Or not."

Victor nodded. "I get sinking the car. But why not just load the boat back up and take it home with him? Why try to sink it? Why sink the trailer?"

"Because that way the only evidence is at the bottom of the lake. When he arrived at the fishing camp, he would have immediately hidden his boat and sunk the trailer and then joined up with Tom to go out fishing with him every day. That way he thinks we're thrown off his trail of having the means to get from the fishing camp to the Flatwoods without someone hearing his truck start up at night. This killer likes to get rid of any evidence by using water. Esau in the shower. Salem in the lake. Trying to sink the boat."

"So it's just a coincidence that Salem shows up at the fishing camp while Noble is there even though he barely associates with his son?"

"No. I told you, I don't believe in coincidences," Dave said. He had thought all this through with Sheila the night before as they bounced ideas off one another. "Noble is the one who called Salem and told him that Celeste had brought money to Esau. Anonymously, I'm sure. But he called him all the same. He must have snuck up to Esau's cottage after he saw Celeste arrive, seen the whole thing. We know he went to the store that morning; Tom told me that, assuming he only went for lunchmeat to take out fishing. But that was just an excuse to call Salem and lure him there."

"Well, then, there's still the coincidence of her bringing the money."

"I'll give you that," Dave said, not seeing any way around it. "But Noble would've lured him down there no matter what. Or maybe he brought the boat so he could get to the Campbell mansion by water, sneak up the hill and kill them all in the night. One way or another, this was all premeditated. Had to be."

The river meandered away now and the valley widened a bit. They were coming into what would pass as a congested area for Fogtown: a church and a post office across the road from the house where the post mistress and her husband lived. Other than that, the only signs of life were driveways that shot off the dirt road that served as the main road for the area. Beyond these drives were mostly farms that stretched out along the bottomlands of the Big Laurel River, pastures rich with sediment from the old river. But other drives shot up mountains to the homes of the people who relished being as far away as they could get from everyone, many of them people who had been born before the turn of the century and weren't keen on the larger world that had been brought to them by radio, television, and two world wars, not to mention the trouble their sons had faced in their travels to fight in Korea.

Victor turned off one such driveway, little more than two tire tracks that cut through the woods. At the end of this drive a rusty mailbox leaned on a lichen-covered post. The name BOGGS had been written on the box ages ago, the white letters now smudged and faded. Brambles and trees grew so close on either side that they ran their scratching tips down the sides of Victor's cruiser. There were bursts of reddish-orange in the trees from where the trumpet vines had snaked their way up to more sunlight and were now in bloom. Kudzu covered some of the trees, slowly choking them to death. Most around these parts would have trimmed all of this back in the height of summer, but apparently Noble had allowed it all to run wild. There was a small creek running white over flat, black rocks as they climbed a mountain toward Burgess Noble's house.

The rain increased but still did not develop into a downpour. If not for the task at hand, it would have made for a

Chapter 30

After Victor parked they got out of the car and immediately Victor called out, "Hallo," which was traditional here, a way to announce oneself from the get-go and not be mistaken for a trespasser or someone who meant mischief. Victor's call echoed across the cove into nothingness. Dave was struck by the quiet here. This was a place far back in the hills, but there was not much birdcall. Perhaps the rain had hushed them, but the stillness seemed more eerie than peaceful. He could feel somebody or something watching them. He always felt that way in Fogtown.

Just as they began to walk toward the house, Burgess Noble eased out of the front door and leaned onto the half wall that enclosed the porch.

"How do," he said, as quietly as if they were on the porch with him. "What are you boys doing up here on my land?"

Victor was holding his badge wallet up before him. "Sheriff Burns and Deputy Hendricks." He slid it back into nice late afternoon shower to witness. If not for all of the mess, Dave might have been on his houseboat porch with one eye on a book and the other on the way the thin rain gave slight movement to the still, green water of the lake near the marina. The fog arose from every cleft in the hills, slithering along the creek.

Around a sharp curve and there, on the hillside, was a white clapboard house, recently painted so the white was startling against the lush green of the tree canopy behind it.

the front pocket of his pants and then rested his hand atop the handle of his pistol in its holster at his belt. Dave knew Victor was doing this purposefully and not just out of habit. What Noble couldn't see was that Victor had unlatched the holster before getting out of the car so he could pluck the pistol out easily if he needed to.

Noble stood there, only his torso and head visible to them from their vantage point below the porch.

"We just need to ask you a few more questions, Mr. Noble," Dave said, "and get some things cleared up."

"Y'all can just stay right there," Noble said. "I can hear you just fine."

They both stopped.

"Now what's the question?" Noble asked. Still he stayed back from the edge of the porch so he was partly lost to shadow.

"We need to know your whereabouts Friday morning."

"I was at the fishing camp. I got there Thursday night and never left until Sunday morning."

"Tom Jenkins says you left Friday morning."

"I went to the store and bought lunchmeat and light bread. Ask the clerk."

"Mr. Noble, have you seen or had any contact at all with Patricia Campbell?"

Noble brought his pistol up quick, although it seemed in slow motion to Dave, and fired one shot. The blast was deafening, echoing down the mountainside. Just as Dave's head turned he could see the quick tug back of Victor's right shoulder, the burst of blood flying out behind him.

Victor stumbled backward but did not fall immediately. Dave plucked the pistol from Victor's holster and brought it back around to fire on Noble, but he was gone.

Victor's knees buckled and then gave way so he folded up on the yard. Dave ran around and shoved himself underneath Victor's left shoulder so Victor could half lie upon him and half walk. He shuffled him into the car's back seat. Dave examined the wound enough to see that the bullet had passed through, which was a blessing. There wasn't a tremendous amount of bleeding but enough to concern him, and Victor had a hole that went completely through his upper shoulder.

Victor was grayish-looking and taking deep breaths. "Go get him," he said.

"I've got to get you to a doctor, Victor."

"Call backup and go get him," Victor said through gritted teeth, his eyes clenched shut. Then he roared, louder than Dave had ever heard him: "Hurry the hell up!"

Dave held in the button on the two-way radio and called for any help they could get. He knew that the nearest cop had to be at least a half hour or so away, but as soon as they heard, "Officer down," they'd put the gas to the floor.

"Go, dammit, go get him!" Victor hollered. "And find her."

Dave hunkered down low and zoomed from the cover of the car to the side of the house, expecting a bullet to slice through him at any moment. He put his back to the house and held the gun with both hands in front of himself, easing around to the front porch steps. Only now did he notice that the thin rain had stopped. He raced up the steps and burst into the house. He could hear movement in the back, so he ran through the living room and into the small kitchen just as the back door banged shut. When he reached the door, he saw Noble running away. The rough terrain was not agreeable with his wooden leg and he crashed to the ground, but sprang back up and disappeared into the trees.

Dave had to make the split-second decision to search the house for Patricia or go after him. But there was nothing else to do but to crash into those woods behind Noble; without him they might never find the girl. He bolted out the back door.

Just past a small backyard the mountain was a steep incline downhill. There was a faint path, so faint it was most likely that of a local fox, which cut through the thick laurel bushes rising ten feet about his head. All his life he had heard stories of people getting lost in woods that were overtaken by thickets like these. People called them "laurel hells." They provided an impossible maze to navigate because every direction looked exactly the same. But Dave made sure that he kept going down the hill, as if pulled by the river he knew was at its bottom. All around him the mist rose up like ghosts being released from their graves. The sun was sinking fast, and he knew daylight would be quick behind it. He had to get this done before darkness fell or Noble would be gone forever.

Dave nearly twisted his ankle in a badger hole before pulling it up just in time and stopped abruptly in the hopes of hearing Noble breaking through the limbs. He did. Not straight down the mountain, though, but to the right.

Noble was zigzagging down the mountainside and had a huge advantage over Dave in that he knew this land, most likely as well as the back of his hand. Still, he had the disadvantage of a lost leg that was surely causing him trouble with his maneuvering.

Dave set the safety on the pistol and took off again, running harder, with everything in him, so fast that he feared he might tumble over himself. But he thought of Victor, bleeding in the car. He thought of the young woman, Patricia, most likely tied up somewhere, perhaps injured, hopefully not already dead. He had to keep going, even though the catch in his side was throbbing with the pain of running.

Down, down, toward the river. He stopped and could hear the water's music. He was close to the bottom of the mountain now. And just as he started to take off again, he heard it: Noble jumping into the river, splashing through the shoals.

Dave crashed down as quickly as he could, briars and limbs tearing at his face and hands. He felt wetness in his palm and unclenched his fingers to find a dark red bubble there. He realized he had been cut from grabbing hold of some big-thorned vine with too much force a few yards back.

And there was the river, shimmering and peaceful, so shallow here that he could see every stone on its floor. He stood in the trees at its edge, careful to not reveal himself. As soon as he eased out of the woods and stepped in the river, a shot rang out. He knew Noble would expect him to hunker down and stay still, so instead he barreled back up onto the bank where he would have at least a little cover and ran toward the sound of the gun. He held the pistol out in front of him and moved low and fast, maneuvering as carefully as he could over tree roots and mossy rocks.

He stopped. Something in his gut told him Noble was near. Hiding. Waiting. He could feel him the same way he could feel that old evil breathing out of the mountainside. Maybe that's why bad things had happened here so often. Had the bad things created the evil, or had the evil given birth to the bad things? Dave didn't know, but he knew he wanted to get the hell out of here.

"Tell me where the girl is, Noble! She hasn't done anything to deserve this."

"They all deserve it!" Noble called back. He was close. Too close for comfort, in fact.

"Even if you shoot me, this is over, and you know it. Every cop in Southern Kentucky and Middle Tennessee is headed this way, Noble. If you give it up now, it'll be in your favor."

"You think I care what happens to me? I quit caring about that a long time ago." He certainly sounded authentic. "Salem's father ruined my father's life and then Salem ruined mine. What goes around comes around."

A shot zipped by Dave's ear so closely that he thought at first it had taken his lobe with it. A chunk of leaves the bullet had torn through came to rest on his shoulder. He grabbed frantically at the side of his head and when he held his hands out before him he was startled by the blood he saw before remembering it was only from the briars.

Noble took this moment of discombobulation to burst through the laurel and grab Dave from behind, his arm firmly clenched around Dave's neck and the unmistakable cold-like-no-other-cold of the pistol barrel against his temple.

"Let's end this right here," Noble said, his breath playing at the top of Dave's head. "Why shouldn't I?"

"Because I'm more like you than them," Dave said, calm and low. "My family always earned everything on their own. Didn't steal or cheat anybody. Just worked like dogs their whole lives."

Noble pulled back the hammer on the pistol, the small sound deafening in Dave's ears.

"I don't give a good goddamn about any of it any—" Noble said but then Dave drew his elbow so sharply back into Noble's stomach that his breath left him.

Noble's arm holding his pistol flew high and he squeezed the trigger, the shot so loud that Dave couldn't hear anything but the shot as he swung around and threw his forehead against Noble's nose.

He put all of his might—his rage, maybe—into his right hand as he grasped Noble's wrist, beating it against a rock until he felt the bone shatter and the pistol clattered to the ground.

Noble let out a jagged howl of pain, then gritted his teeth.

Dave was like a wild animal, so full of adrenaline that he felt he could have picked up Noble and held him over his head. Instead he threw Noble over onto his belly and grabbed his arms—Noble squalling again when Dave took hold of his broken wrist—and quick as lighting a match Dave knocked the cuffs against his leg so they'd open, slid them onto Noble's arms, locked them, then jumped up to stand over Noble, breathing hard.

"Tell me where the girl is."

"At the bottom of the lake," Noble spat, but Dave wasn't convinced.

"Why ruin your life like this? For what?"

"If you want me to talk then get me off my belly."

Dave grabbed hold of Noble and turned him over, positioned him against a tree. Noble glared at him, breathing hard for a moment before speaking. "I was avenging my grandfather. And my father."

"Your stepfather, you mean. Waylon Boggs."

"He was an evil bastard, but he was the only father I ever had. The whole time he was dying, he told me what a disappointment I was for never getting justice for him. Over and over. I sat there and listened and when he died, I got up and decided to do something about it. Salem and Esau deserved what they got. I hope they're in hell right now."

Then somehow Noble slid forward in a flash and kicked the toe of his boot into Dave's ankle, causing his leg to crumple. Noble had misjudged, though, and slid back down, crashing heavily into the brush. Dave fell to the rocky ground and felt a bolt of electricity run up his back from where his tailbone had connected with a jagged rock, but before Noble could get to him, he kicked the sole of his boot into the man's face, crushing his nose. Noble collapsed on his back, blood streaming over his lips.

They both laid there, breathing hard for only a moment with nothing except the sound of the shallow river wending its way toward the lake. Then Dave hustled Noble to his feet and directed him back up the mountain. He couldn't help but think how this was a human being as he walked behind him with his eyes on Noble's neck, the fingers of his left hand sunk deep into the meat of Noble's arm while the other hand held the pistol up. He hoped Noble wouldn't try to fight him again, that he wouldn't have to use the gun on this man. Dave had had enough of killing way back in Europe, and the recent murders had made him more certain of this. Noble had slaughtered two people in cold blood, but he was still a person himself. Being human and also being a monster was the hardest part to rectify.

By the time they reached Noble's house, the wail of sirens greeted them.

Chapter 31

Noble had not hurt the girl beyond the roughness it took to get her still enough to tie the rope around her hands and feet, beyond the trauma of having a large rag shoved into her mouth and then more rope around her face so she couldn't spit it out. That was enough. But he had not hurt her other than that, Patricia told him.

By the time Dave had gotten back up the mountain the ambulance had arrived from Albany, but the other police officers were still rushing in. Dave found the girl in the root cellar, tied to a chair in the complete darkness, surrounded by jars of food that looked like they had been preserved decades ago. He noticed a whole shelf of kraut that had turned a muddy brown, another shelf of canned tomatoes that had started to waste away into nothing more than blood-red membranes in their own juice.

Patricia was trembling as he cut off the ropes. He had never felt so sorry for anyone as he was when he pulled the nasty rag from her mouth. She choked and coughed and tears ran down her face, but she did not weep. He could tell she was a strong young woman. Probably anything that had been good in Salem Campbell had ended up in his daughter, and she had nearly lost her life because of his wrongdoings and because of her grandfather's offenses, which Dave would still have to find out about.

"You're all right now," he said, and she fell against him, exhausted. Never before had he so regretted not having a child as in that moment.

"I thought he was going to kill me," she said, hoarse. Dave did not say back to her that he very well might have as soon as he had thought up some elaborate staging for it like he had done for her half brother and father.

"Come on, let's get you home to your mother," Dave said.

He drove Victor's cruiser back and had Patricia sit up front with him. He followed the ambulance carrying Victor down the mountain and back to the small hospital in Shady Grove. Patricia would need to be looked over, too, no matter how much she protested. Collins had wrestled Noble into the back of his cruiser. He'd have a field day out of telling everyone he had been the one to bring him back, most likely conveniently leaving out that Dave had been the one to capture him.

The young woman looked out the window the entire way back, her face as blank as a sheet of typing paper. No emotion on it at all.

"How did he get you?"

"He was waiting, at our driveway. He must have known I'd be coming home for my mother. Just as I turned into the driveway, he came walking out of the woods and stood in the middle of the road, his hands out in front of him like he was hurt or something. I rolled my window down to see what was the matter, and he ripped the door open and pushed his way in. Blindfolded me, tied me up. And that was it. I thought sure he'd kill me."

"Did he say anything to you?"

She gave a little disgusted laugh, not unlike the habit her mother had of preceding some sentences this way. "He talked the entire way. Nonstop. Told me everything wrong my father and grandfather had done in their lives."

"Which was?"

"He said my family got rich off his land. Said my grandfather claimed a property dispute and took all their land, back in the early 1900s, just before the timber boom. Cut down all the trees his grandfather grew up with and made a fortune that allowed my father his career in politics, his wealth. Then, years later, my father took the only woman he ever loved. My mother. He was obsessed with her, I guess. All these years."

"Land or love," Dave said aloud, but she didn't ask him to explain. *Sometimes both*, he thought.

"I thought for sure he was going to kill me after he told me all about his stepfather. There was this look that came over him. It was like his whole face changed. He said that man took all of his anger out on him and his mother. But it was like he didn't blame his stepfather half as much for that as he blamed *my* family. That's when I was terrified," she said. "I thought for sure he'd kill me. And then y'all came." Her voice caught so she stopped talking and turned back to watching the passing landscape.

He didn't ask Patricia more; he wanted her to rest. After a while, she did. She laid her head back and closed her eyes without going to sleep and there was a comfortable silence between them in the car. Once she was asleep he sat crooked in his seat to keep the pressure off his bruised tailbone, which was throbbing. But he hadn't wanted to let on in front of her. Nothing a little aspirin wouldn't relieve.

At the hospital, he went in to fetch a wheelchair for Patricia. She didn't seem to need it but he wasn't taking any chances; protocol seemed to call for as much. He wheeled her in and was allowed to stay with her. They were taken to the emergency room where four metal beds were separated by wall curtains that didn't quite meet. He sat by Patricia's bed—she didn't want to lie down but not long after she did, she dozed off from her exhaustion—and watched Victor in his bed across from them. The space between his curtains was only a few inches, but Dave was sitting right where he could see Victor's head propped on the pillows. His shoulder had been well-bandaged and he had been given a shot that had quickly lulled him into rest as well.

Dave heard heels on the emergency room floor, rushing, pausing when they neared the space Victor inhabited. And then, there was Janet, dressed to the nines like she had just left a cocktail party.

Janet leaned over Victor and kissed him. On the lips, on the eyes, on the forehead. She loved Victor in a way she had never loved Dave, he could see. It wasn't just some fling, then. They loved each other. He had never considered this possibility before. He had always just thought of their relationship as a betrayal, as a way to hurt him. But it had not been about him at all, and he could see that now. Wrong as they had gone about it, they really loved each other. Dave was surprised to find no malice in himself at this realization. In some way this made it all easier, better.

He had not been the best husband to her. He had not loved her properly, fully. He had always loved the job more. He had always loved everything more, really. Driving alone, singing with the radio. Fishing with Rex. Listening to music. He didn't know why. Something between them had never completely latched and he saw now that it was not his fault, nor hers. Just life.

Then, another set of small heels, rushing toward them. The curtain was ripped back by a bejeweled hand and there was Celeste Campbell. She ran in and took hold of Patricia's hands, rousing her, kissing her fingers.

"It's all right, Mama," Patricia said, her voice still weak. "I'm fine."

Celeste kissed her daughter's hands once more, then turned to him with unshed tears in her eyes. "Thank you, Deputy," she said. "They told me—you saved her."

Chapter 32

After the supper Rex made for them, they went down to Dave's houseboat to sit on the porch and have drinks since he had a better view of the lake. The Milky Way was bright tonight over the black water, and Dave turned off all the lights on the boat so they could see the stars better. After a few minutes, their eyes adjusted to the darkness enough that they could see one another easily. Dave put a Hank Williams album on the record player. Rex made his perfect gin and tonic using the Tanqueray and rosemary he had brought along. The drinks tasted like summer in a glass, and every time they refilled, they had a new toast.

"Now don't cuss me out, Dave, but I think we should hoist a toast to Victor," Rex said. "He may have had a rougher day than any of us."

Dave held his glass up, smiling.

"A toast to Victor's health, then," Rex said, and clinked glasses all around. "Cheers."

"Cheers," Dave said. "They said he'll heal up just fine, but it'll take a while."

"He's lucky," Nina said.

"Can you talk about what Noble said once you got him back to the office?"

"As long as it doesn't end up in the newspaper," Dave said, cutting his eyes at Nina.

"I only report what you say is on the record."

"Well, this is all *off* the record," Dave said. "Promise?"

Nina nodded. "Of course."

"He told us some of this and research found some of it, thanks to Sheila. This case being cracked is due to her research."

"We need to have another drink so we can toast Sheila, then," Rex said, and they all laughed.

"Oldest story in the world, really. Just like you said, Rex. Most crimes in these parts happen over land or love. In this case it *was* both."

Rex nodded.

"Noble was eighteen years old when Celeste broke up with him. When he pursued her, Celeste's father gave him a good talking-to. Noble already wanted away from his stepfather so that was the nudge he needed to get the hell out of here. He was raised fishing the Big Laurel, so he went to Memphis and got a job on one of the big catfish boats. We're going to follow his tracks to see what else he might have done over the years. I don't think a killer like this just goes his whole life without being violent."

"Not in my experience," Nina said.

"But if he was just a fisherman then why the scripture being used at the murders? Was he religious?" Rex asked.

"No, but his stepfather was a fanatical preacher. He drilled all those scriptures into Noble's head and when the man got sick, Noble came back here to be with him as he was dying. Even though he'd been so mean to him. On his deathbed, Boggs told him what a disappointment he was, for never avenging the way the Campbell family had wronged him."

"Let's back up to Salem's father. How had he been part of it?" Rex asked.

"As crooked as Salem was, his father was even worse and had filed false claims against Boggs, who later became Noble's stepfather. Boggs owned some of the best bottomland in the state. And Old Man Campbell took it away from them. This pretty much ruined Noble's family. Left them with about a tenth of the huge acreage they had owned, turning Boggs mean, and so on. Noble's real father died when Noble was a baby, so the only father he ever knew was Boggs."

"And the grudge against Salem was just because of his father?" Nina asked.

"No," Dave said. "In high school Noble is good-looking, tall, a star basketball player, pushing through his family misery back home. And he gets the prettiest girl at school."

"Celeste," Nina said.

"Right. Becomes too possessive, figures Celeste to not be the firecracker she is, and she won't put up with his shit. Quits him and never looks back. Her father jumps him, he leaves for the riverboat, etc. He has no idea Celeste has even married Salem Campbell until he comes home when Boggs is dying. After Boggs is buried, Noble doesn't do anything but sit and study about how he'll get revenge on the Campbell family, avenge his stepfather. He goes to the fishing camp three or four times, waiting for the perfect opportunity, and finally he makes it happen on his own."

"What made for that?"

"Celeste took Esau money to pay his debt to Frank White. Salem came shortly thereafter. Noble went to the store—the closest phone—under the guise of buying food for lunch not long after Celeste left, so he must have called Salem and told him that he had witnessed Celeste giving Esau money."

"But why would Salem get into a boat with Noble?" Rex asked.

"He didn't have a choice. After Noble heard Salem arguing with his son, he waited until Salem rushed out and ran up behind him, shoved a pistol in his back and tied him up just like he did Patricia. Put a gag in his mouth, pistol whipped him, and kept him in his cottage until late that night, when he took him out in the boat, rowing all the way up into the Flatwoods, which he knew was the most remote part of the lake. Stabbed him and threw his body overboard. His big mistake was killing him in the boat of course, because we found the presence of blood, which tied it to the crime. Noble rowed back to the camp and tried to sink the boat. Knocked a big hole in the hull and weighed it down with rocks and dirt. But he was in too big a hurry, and the one thing he couldn't control was the weather. The storm was so bad the next day that it caused the boat to rise up. He had knocked the hole too far up, so it didn't sink again on its own."

"So we were right in thinking it had drifted to Catfish Cove from this side of the lake," Rex said.

"*You* were right about that, yes," Dave said, calling Rex out on his modesty.

"He confessed this?" Nina asked.

"Yes," Dave said. "It was almost like he was proud of it. Still, even if he hadn't, this would have been a hole in one because we had him tied to the boat."

"How so?" Rex asked.

"He had worn his fishing apron from his days on the Mississippi to keep blood off him. The apron was at his house. But when he lifted Salem to put him over the side of the boat, blood covered the apron. I could tell it easily, but the luminol test will prove it."

"But can luminol tell the difference between human blood and fish blood, which would be all over the apron, too?" Nina asked.

"Luminol can't, but a microscope can once luminol reveals blood has been there, even after it's washed away."

"So then he waited a whole day before he killed Esau," Rex said. "To further punish the family. And he was going to kill Patricia next?"

"Probably. To hurt Celeste as much as he could."

"But writing that scripture at the scenes and all that—" Nina said, then stopped, as if trying to arrange her words properly.

"What?" Dave asked.

"Did he do that because he's crazy, or because he just wanted it to seem like a crazy person?"

"It would take a madman to do what he did," Rex said.

"I don't know about that, Rex," Dave said. "I don't think he was so much out of his mind as he was just full of vengeance that turned into pure meanness." He didn't say how he believed Fogtown could conjure that in a person, or at least prod it. "He was a cruel, violent man. When we look at his record it's all quiet, but Celeste never reported how he hurt her. I'm sure other women didn't, either. And who knows what else he got away with while he went up and down the river?"

"Land or love," Rex said. "You're right. In this case it was both. If "love" is the right word for the way he felt about Celeste."

"More about control and power than love," Dave said.

"You'd be amazed at how many men think those are all the same thing," Nina said, and drained the last of her cocktail. "But how did you know it was him, Dave?"

"Once we saw that he had a connection to Celeste, all the pieces went together. It was like I could see the puzzle laid out before me, with that one missing piece. He had already said things to me that were pieces. Then Sheila found that his stepfather was one of the people who had been ripped off by Salem's father. And one piece after another. It all added up. Motive, opportunity, timeline. It had to be him."

"Esau's cottage was ransacked, though. Ever figure out why?"

"I think he was probably looking for information on Salem's daughter. Her address. While he was in there he also took Esau's pistol and all his money. Revenge was at the forefront of his mind."

"Do you want another G and T, love?" Rex asked Nina.

"I *want* another, but I best not. I have to work early in the morning, boys." Nina stood and stretched her arms high in the air as the bones in her shoulders popped. "In case you didn't hear, there's a big murder trial coming up and I'm the lead reporter now."

Nina hugged Dave from behind as she passed. "I'm proud of you, buddy," she said. "Even as a little girl I always knew you'd be one of the good guys."

"You're a good one, Nina," he said.

"I know," she smiled, and kissed him on the top of his head. She tousled Rex's hair. "Good night, you," she said. Rex smacked his lips together in an air kiss for her. She stepped over the railing onto her houseboat porch and slid the door shut behind her.

"I should turn in, too," Rex said. "I was thinking of going back out to the Sungranny Spot tomorrow. Want to join me?"

"Sounds good to me," Dave said.

"Early morning or in the evening?"

"You know I love to go out in the cool of the day."

"Evening it is." Rex rose slowly from his seat, bones popping. "I sound like the bloody Tin Man," he said, and they laughed. "I'm glad to see the old Dave back," he said. "That gloomy and angry Dave I've been with for the past year wasn't as much fun."

"Thanks for hanging in there with me, Rex. I appreciate it more than I can say."

"Always will, my lad," he said, and took the shortcut back to the walkway through Dave's boat.

Just as he left, Nina came back out onto her houseboat porch and stood in the shadows. "I can't go to sleep without first telling you that I forgive you for suspecting I had something to do with this," she said.

"Only briefly," Dave said. "I wouldn't be a good detective otherwise. Got to consider everybody."

"But do you know *why* you couldn't trust me?"

Dave didn't reply. He thought he knew, but he wasn't sure he could articulate it just yet.

"Because I'm not like any woman you've ever known before. I'm freer, wilder, not so confined by what the world tells me I need to be because I'm a woman," she said. "And that scares the hell out of men."

"Maybe you're right," Dave said.

"I am absolutely right," she said forcibly, but with a smile in her voice. "Good night." She slipped back into the houseboat and slid shut her door.

Dave looked up at the night sky. So many stars there was more silver than blue-black. That clean cedar smell of Cedar Lake washed over his face and all felt right with the world for him. The record player had gone off and all the little living things in the trees and water had revved up for a late-night chorus. Crickets, katydids, whippoorwills, frogs, cicadas. But then, he heard someone pecking at the front door of his houseboat. Nobody on the Marie really knocked. They usually burst in whenever they wanted to. Maybe Rex had forgotten something and had accidentally locked the door behind him. Dave rushed through and snatched it open.

There stood Vashti Bryant in a sundress decorated with little daisies. He couldn't help looking at the beauty of her collarbone.

"Well, hey there," he said. "Wasn't expecting you."

"You said to drop in for a drink sometime," she said. "Seemed like tonight would be a good time for that after the day you had."

"Come on through," he said, and held the door open wide.

She followed him out onto the porch where the wide lake and the wide sky greeted them, so magnificent Vashti had to acknowledge it. "Well, look at that," she said.

"Have a seat and let me get you a drink. Gin and tonic or Irish whiskey?"

"Got any Jameson's?"

"My favorite," he said.

She raised her eyebrows and nodded.

He poured her a couple fingers of the whiskey and held up his glass. "Here's to us," he said.

"Cheers," Vashti said, and as if they had planned it, both of them took a drink in unison then tilted their heads back to study the stars.

Whatever evil lurked in the mountains and hollows of Fogtown or the hard hearts of murderers, that sky was its opposite. Sitting here like this with Cedar Lake before them was, too.

Acknowledgments

I am indebted to my agent, Joy Harris, whom I trust and love.

I am thankful to the entire Crooked Lane team, who have been so wonderful to work with, especially my editor, Sara Henry, who tightened and improved this novel, as well as Thai Fantauzzi Perez, Julia Abbott, and everyone else who has worked to bring this book to the world.

My writing community is so dear to me, and I'm especially thankful to early readers Alice Hale Adams, Greta McDonough, and Kathi Whitley, all among my favorite people and astute readers. David Arnold, Gavin Colton, and Johnny Lackey: I can't thank you enough. Kevin Gardner and Tim Groninger go to the lake with me and are always willing to celebrate with me.

I'm thankful to have parents and close family who have supported me and encouraged me as an artist ever since I was a child. They also took me to the lakes of Kentucky and Tennessee, which inspired Cedar Lake for this book.

Everything I do is for Jason and my children.